Hunter James Dolin

The Half-Breed Gunslinger II

Bret Lee Hart

Hunter James Dolin
The Half-Breed Gunslinger II

HUNTER JAMES DOLIN
The Half-Breed Gunslinger II

Hunter James Dolin survived the revenge war of Myakka City, Florida, by killing the men who raised their guns against him and his loved ones – all but one.

The Governor directed the Army to investigate, forcing the Half-Breed Gunslinger to seek refuge deep in the swamps of the Everglades.

Hunter James Dolin was content to live the rest of his life in solitude – 'til he was sought out and told of the whereabouts of the one that got away.

This would spark a new battle of revenge, overshadowed by the Civil War, but not soon forgotten by the people who inhabit the Florida swamplands.

❧ * ☙

PROLOGUE

The year was 1862 and the War Between the States was raging in full, pitting countrymen against countrymen. Florida was the third of the original seven states to secede from the Union. There had been few battles fought there to this point, due to the state's remote location and small population. Florida's most important role was as a food supplier of beef cattle and salt for the Confederate Army.

The Union armies had strongholds in North and Central Florida, and as far South as Key West, but the soldiers avoided the treacherous swamps in the everglades. Only Indians and Crackers dared enter these cypress wet lands – crawling with gators, bears, venomous snakes, wild boars, and mosquitoes – relentless and numerous.

Hunter James Dolin easily made these swamps his refuge, for he was both of these, half-white and half-Injun, what the people of these parts called a *Half-Breed*. He was born without a family as his mother had died giving birth to him, and his father had moved on long before.

Hunter was raised as the slave of a small Lower Creek Seminole Indian Tribe. He escaped at a young age to the north, where he learned the ways of the white man. He mastered the use of Sam Colt's revolver and took a liking to gambling, preferably poker. Hunter had a skill for the game of cards, or maybe he was just lucky – he did not know – but what he did know was that men did not give up their money easily.

After killing three men on three separate occasions, he had built up a reputation as a gunfighter. Most white men could not accept the fact that a dirty *half-breed* could beat them at cards without cheating. With the pressure building on him, he felt that itch to go west, where he landed a job with the Union Army as a tracker and killer of the feared Comanche, and any other savages that got in the white man's way. Hunter James did this for several years 'til he heard his father, who he had still not met, had returned to Florida. Hunter worked his way back home, only to find his pa had been murdered, shot in the back by a cowardly soul.

He tried to settle down in the cabin left to him by his father, a retired soldier turned gunfighter, who went by the name James Dolin. Hunter had fallen in love with a beautiful woman named Lilith, and cared for a young boy named Zeke, and he swore to the heavens they would all be together as a family. But they were killed by the same men who killed his pa, along with some others. His lovely Lilith was shot in the head, and the boy died from fever, a result of a beating.

His only friend left in this world, Matt, was killed in a gun battle in the town of Myakka. Matt was an older man who became a father figure to Hunter for the short time they knew each other. He had given the gunslinger a job at the saloon as a peacekeeper, and fought beside him to his death.

Hunter James Dolin's revenge had been justified – he killed thirty to forty men, and burned Myakka City down to the ground. But, that was the past, we must now move on to the present.

Chapter One

It was a hot summer day in late June or maybe early July, who knew? There weren't too many calendars in these parts, these parts being an island located in the center of the Everglades, three days ride south of Lake Okeechobee. Here is where for some time Hunter James Dolin had stayed in solitude amongst the saw-grass marshes, where he stayed in what the Seminole Indians called a *Chickee*. The platform house was built of logs that stood three feet off the ground for protection from flooding and animals. The roof was slanted and made of green woven palm fronds. There were no solid walls between the posts, for the Indians of the swamp were always on the move; perhaps they could see no reason for building any.

Late in the afternoon, Hunter sat in front of a modest fire on a crude stool he had carved out of a Cypress stump. He was chewing on a cooked baby gator tail when he saw the riders coming toward him across the green, wet prairie. It was damn near impossible to sneak up on his small tropical hardwood hammock, actually a raised limestone island, surrounded in all directions by the ankle-deep water and knee-high grass that went on for miles.

Hunter wore his gunbelt which held his set of Colt 44 revolvers, and his sawed off double-barreled shotgun lay across his lap. As their horses walked closer toward him, he could see they were white men.

They were still a quarter of a mile off, the smoke from his fire guiding them to his position.

He had not seen anyone in many months; even the Seminoles didn't travel this deep into the marsh very often; and if they did, they avoided the Half-Breed. They believed he was possessed by an evil spirit, which meant bad magic followed him were ever he went. The Indians called him, *Lus-tee Manito Nak-Nee*, which translates to 'black spirit man'.

Hunter finished his meal, throwing the bones into the fire. The men were close now; the wake in the water from the movement of the horses' legs could be heard as well as seen. He recognized these men from a long ago poker game, in a faraway saloon, in a city that was no more. He remembered these old veterans as being friendly, but time has a way of changing things; Hunter trusted no one.

He broke open the shotgun, checking to make sure it was loaded. This was purely out of habit; his guns were always cleaned and loaded and ready to fire; he cocked both hammers back, resting it again on his lap. He then un-holstered his right handed revolver and spun the cylinder up by his ear, stopping it with a double click of his thumb. With his right finger on the Colt's trigger and his left finger on the shotgun trigger, he waited patiently for them to arrive.

The old men came to a halt in the shin-high swamp water. A water moccasin swam by in front of their horses, spooking them just a bit. They looked uneasily around; there was nothing but grass and swamp. Staring hard at the little island they could now see someone sitting next to a fire, the smoke rising straight up, for there was little to no wind.

"Wat chyah think, Jebediah?"

"Hell, I don't know, Walt." Jebediah stretched his neck forward, his eyes squinting as he tried to focus on the man at the fire.

"It's got to be him, who else could live way the devil out here?"

"Well, I reckon we need to ride in, at least in speakin' distance, yah' think?" Walt asked nervously.

"I spose," agreed Jebediah. "We're already in rifle distance the way that son shoots. If he wanted us dead, we'd done been shot already."

"Let's do what we came to do then," replied Walt. "Can't live forever."

They began moving their horses slowly, the grass parting for them as they went; the sound of the water could be heard sloshing off their hooves. As they got closer, the old men could now see that it was the gunslinger, his shoulder length, jet-black hair hanging down from underneath his black brimmed hat. The old crackers came to a halt twenty feet from him making sure their hands were in clear sight. There was silence and a long pause, making Walt a bit uncomfortable.

Jebediah finally broke that silence, "Howdy, Mr. Dolin, 'member us?"

Hunter said nothing; he just glared at the two men with his piercing steel-blue eyes.

Walt broke in, after involuntarily clearing his throat, "We three had a friendly card game at Matt's saloon a ways back, in Myakka city. It's a shame 'bout Matt – he was a good man and a good friend."

"What do you want?" asked Hunter.

"We came to warn yah, son," explained Jebediah. "The army has put a bounty on your head."

"You called me son," said Hunter.

Walt looked at Jebediah uneasily, Jeb answered, "Sorry 'bout that. I didn't mean to offend."

"No fault taken," explained Hunter, "Matt used to call me that."

The gunslinger released the hammer on his revolver and put it back into its holster. He then did the same with the shotgun, releasing the triggers and leaning it against a small palm tree conveniently within arm's reach.

"Please join me for some food; I got some mighty sweet gator meat on the spit. You can tether the horses up here on the lime rock behind me," Hunter pointed over his shoulder with his thumb, "under the cypress trees next to the Appaloosa."

"Well, all righty then," said Walt. He looked to Jebediah. "See, I told you he weren't crazy."

"Shut up, Walt; I didn't say no such thing."

The two old veterans could be heard bickering as they walked their horses out of the swampy water up into the trees. They returned a few minutes later, still bickering at one another; Jebediah had a bottle of whiskey in his mitts.

"This here is good Kentucky bourbon," announced Jebediah, as he and Walt pulled up log stumps to sit upon, "from Kentucky," he added.

"He knows where Kentucky bourbon comes from, you old fool," said Walt with a frown. "Would you like a snort there, Hunter James?"

The gunslinger picked up a tin cup from the ground and blew into it, removing an oak leaf and some dust; he then tossed it to Jebediah.

"That would be better than a stick whoopin'," said Hunter. "I done run out of hooch a ways back."

"How long you been without?" asked Walt, as Jebediah leaned over handing Hunter his tin, which was now full to the rim with the Kentucky brew.

"It's been about twenty settin's of the sun, I'd say."

"Damn!" exclaimed Walt, "that's a long time; you're a better man than I."

Jebediah nodded his head in agreement.

Hunter continued with his arms up, showing the men their surroundings. "If you all take a look around yah, you will see there ain't no saloons here 'bouts."

The three men drank and talked as the sun was setting. Normally Hunter would not burn a fire at night for the light could be seen miles out, but the gunslinger was enjoying the company and considered this a special occasion. They began talking about the destruction of Myakka City which turned the conversation more cumbersome.

Matt had been a good friend to Walt and Jebediah, and a fatherly figure to Hunter. They knew Hunter had returned to Florida in hopes of meeting his father for the first time, only to find out he had been murdered. The old timers also knew that Mat, and everyone else around these parts had suspected a rancher named Frank Lugar had done it. This was the first time Hunter had spoken to anyone about anything, not to mention what really happened in the city of Myakka.

In a monotone voice, the gunslinger told his guests of a lovely woman named Lilith and an orphan boy who they had figured to adopt for their own. Their plans were thwarted by Richard Montgomery, a powerful and murderous man. Montgomery and Frank Lugar, along with their hired gunmen, teamed up to destroy the half-breed and his new family. These bad men managed to kill Matt, Lilith, and the boy before the gunslinger killed all of them. With the city burned to the ground, along with Lugar's ranch, Hunter retreated deep into the swamps, finding a home on this small lime rock where he now lived in total isolation.

Walt and Jebediah sat quietly, smoking cigars and listening to their host's story without interruption. After Hunter had finished, the three sat in silence for a long moment. Only the crackling of the fire and the constant buzz of swamp bugs could be heard, until Jebediah finally spoke,

"That's a tragedy, son, if I'd ever heard one. And I have no doubt you speak the truth, but that's not the story been' told out yonder."

"Who's tellin' what?" asked Hunter, "I killed them all, there was no one left to talk."

"Sure 'bout that?" asked Walt. "One a' Lugar's men got away, along with a Chinese; he was the cook or somethin'."

"Yup, I recall," replied Hunter, "I had put the thought of the man that got away from my mind. I never knew about the Chinaman."

Jebediah threw his cigar butt in the fire and pulled a swig off the whiskey bottle. His head shook with a shivering motion from the potent liquor.

"Well?" asked Walt impatiently, "you gonna' tell him what the man's been sayin', or you gonna' jump around like a polecat caught in a beaver trap?"

"I'm gittin' to it, you old fool."

This was no laughing matter, for their talks were drudging up bad memories for Hunter, but then again he was actually being entertained. These two carrying on reminded him of a comic play he saw once in a town in Missouri, when he was a much younger man. So he sat patiently waiting to get the rest of the story.

The old coots finally settled down, and Jebediah continued.

"The one that got away claimed a small war party of Indians attacked the city of Myakka and then Lugar's ranch."

Hunter interrupted, "What's that horseshit story got to do with me?"

Walt picked the story up were Jebediah left off, "He said the leader of this war party was a half-breed, name of Dolin – Hunter James Dolin."

"Find this so called war party," said Hunter, "and question them to find out the truth."

"The Army did just that," replied Jebediah. "They captured a Miccosukee Injun called Raging Bear. He denied knowin' ya', sayin' he was the leader."

The gunslinger stood, and put another log on the fire.

"The blue coats didn't believe the red man with the tomahawk scar on his face, did they?" asked Hunter.

The old timers looked at each other, their mouths slightly open. "You knew Raging Bear?"

"I had run-ins with him, a time or two."

"Well, I hope he weren't your friend, 'cause they shot him, and his braves; Death by firin' squad."

"So they're still lookin' for me." stated Hunter, as he lit a cigar with a burning stick he dug out of the fire.

"No, son," said Jebediah, "the Army's gone back up north. I don't know if you know it or not, but the War Between the States has started. They have done put five hundred dollars on your head before they left and there's bounty hunters lookin' to collect."

Hunter James had heard enough talk for one night and decided to turn in for some shut-eye. He told the old boys they were welcome to stay the night, but they should leave in the morning. The gunslinger did not want them involved in his mess. It didn't seem right to sleep in the one man *Chickee* when he had company, so he bedded down outside under the Cypress.

Staring at the stars for a while seemed to help him make up his mind. He was tired of hiding and looking over his backside, so he would go inland and clear his name, or die trying.

CHAPTER TWO

Hunter woke an hour before sunrise like he always did, his internal clock working like it always had.

Jebediah and Walt had already packed up and gone. This concerned the gunslinger, for he should have heard them leave. Apparently, the liquor affected him causing a deep slumber; he was lucky his enemies were nowhere near. Luck seemed to follow men and it didn't matter what they did or where they did it, what mattered was whether the luck was good or bad. Bad luck always followed good luck eventually, that's just the way it was.

The half-breed gunslinger packed up what little food he had and dressed for the journey. The one thing he did have plenty of was ammunition; of course, this day and age you could never have enough lead. Dressed all in black, he buckled down the gunbelt that held the Colt 44 revolvers before strapping on the side-shoulder holster containing the double-barrel sawed-off shotgun. The thirteen-inch Bowie knife was then tucked into the front of his belt before sliding into his light colored elk skin jacket, the leather fringe dangling from his long arms resembling a bird in flight. He grabbed his rifle and mounted his Appaloosa after putting on his black, wide brimmed hat. The rifle slid into the saddle sheath; loaded, checked, and ready for battle just like all his other weapons he carried.

The gunslinger and his horse he named Zeke, after the ten-year-old boy that Hunter could not save, headed for the so-called civilization. It seemed strange to him calling the Appaloosa Zeke, but it was still somehow fitting; the only reminisce of his past he could deal with at this time.

The horse's legs sloshed through the shin-deep water and parted the knee-high grasses; this went on for miles, until they made it to dry land. The horse and rider then picked up the pace to a gallop. They were heading for Myakka City, the last place on earth Hunter thought he would ever go. It had been about a year since he burned that town to the ground and killed every one in it.

All the killings were justified in his eyes, and would be for most men of these times, but maybe not in the law's – for he knew the 'good old boy' network was alive and well. He grew tired of these thoughts, and pushed them from his mind as they didn't matter anyhow; the objective was to clear his name so he could stop running.

But first, he must kill that son-of-a-dog who got away, the cowardly liar from his haunted past. He would have to be cautious, with the War Between the States in full bore; he didn't know what side the coward was on. After more thought, he wished he had gotten a name from the old men who had joined him on his rock island.

Hunter slowly pulled back on the reins, bringing Zeke to a trot. He began zig-zagging the horse back and forth 'til he spotted what he sought; Jebediah and Walt's tracks, right where it made sense for them to be. The gunslinger followed, hoping they could answer the question he would ask once he caught up.

The gunslinger tracked the two old men easily, for the soil was wet making the hoof prints deep. The sun was approaching straight up when he came across their horses in front of a small honky-tonk. There were three other mounts tied to the same post, signs of many miles of travel covering their matted and sweaty, short hair.

Hunter dismounted and tied Zeke to the far end of the hitching post putting the other animals between his horse and the front door. The last thing he needed was for Zeke to catch a bullet, leaving him at the mercy of his boots. As he approached the saloon he fought the urge to check his guns before entering, and he did so successfully, for he knew they were ready. He had just gone through them on the road less than an hour ago.

The front door to the building was wood and propped open with a sand filled spittoon, making for an easy entrance. The bright sun coming through the door did not reveal Hunter's identity until he made it to the far end of the bar where he placed his back against the wall. Sunlight beamed from two small barred windows at the rear, and there were a few candles lit here and there on tables in the middle.

As his eyes adjusted to the room, he located Walt and Jebediah playing poker with another man at a far table. Jebediah spotted Hunter. As he did, he put his hand on Walt's arm and stared in that direction. Walt looked up to see the gunslinger being served a beer and a bottle by the portly, unshaved bartender.

Walt and Hunter's eyes met; Walt nodded his head toward the three men drinking at the middle of the bar. They were positioned in-between them and so far the men were paying the gunslinger no mind. They arrived just twenty minutes before he had and were indulging in their drinks.

Hunter sized them up; he had seen bounty hunters before and these three certainly fit the bill. He slammed back his beer and filled his empty shot glass with whiskey from his bottle, which he emptied in one gulp.

"Want more beer?" asked the barkeep.

"I reckin'." replied Hunter.

The fat man grabbed his glass and waddled over to a

large barrel, refilling the mug 'til the foam over flowed, dripping on the dirt floor. On his return, he asked a question Hunter had been asked before.

"You part Injun?" This talk was heard by the man closest to Hunter, who was now giving him some attention.

"Say what?" replied Hunter.

"I make the Injuns drink out back," explained the bartender. "They seems to have trouble holdin' their liquor."

"Well, I take after my white father, he could out drink most."

The big man at the center of the bar, with chin whiskers that ran down to his exaggerated belly interrupted their conversation.

"And who might your father be, there, half-breed?" he asked as he turned to face Hunter, the distance between them about five paces.

"Since you're not from 'round here," replied Hunter, "I don't think you'd know him."

"You're right, half-Injun man, we ain't from 'round here. But we done heard of a half-breed runnin' a gang of savages. Do you know they killed fifty good men and burned down a whole town? Know anythin' 'bout that?"

The other two men realized what was going on; they stepped back from the bar and looked at Hunter, just over and around their big partner's shoulder.

"Yup, I heard that bullshit story," said Hunter, before slamming back a shot. "Those Indians the blue coats executed had nothin' to do with it. The half-breed done it all on his own, and those *good men,* you call 'em, had it comin'."

"Well, boys," said the big man as he laughed an evil, gargled sort of laugh.

"I think we has found the man weez' been lookin' fer. There's five-hundred dollars on your head, *half-breed,* dead or alive."

The three bounty hunters slowly put their hands on the butts of their guns.

Hunter did not make a move; He had one advantage, he was at the corner of the bar which had a three-foot wing made of hardwood plank between him and the three gunmen.

"I ain't much for livin' these days, so I guess it will have to be dead," said Hunter in a calm voice. There was a two-second pause, and then the half-breed gunslinger went into action. He dropped down out of sight behind the three-foot wing of the bar as the bounty hunters were drawing their pistols. Hunter pulled the double-barrel shotgun from its side-shoulder holster. He then side-stepped around the corner, front leg forward in a squatting position, and blasted both barrels at their knees.

The buckshot took out the legs of the fat man, putting him to the ground; the second man caught some shrapnel as well and he tried to hobble quickly to the center of the saloon. The third man was making a move, but he was slow.

After dropping the shotgun, Hunter pulled his Colt and shot him in the heart, making the man's finger go slack, disabling him from pulling the trigger; he fell dead on his face.

The hobbling man decided to run for the door, but he didn't make it; the gunslinger shot him in the back of the head, eliminating his concerns about the small lead balls lodged in his thighs as he fell forward through the open doorway.

The sudden silence in the room seemed to be louder than the booms of the gunfire until the fat man woke. With both legs missing from the knee down, he lay on his stomach yelling in pain. To Hunter's surprise, the front half of the man attempted to crawl toward the front door, leaving his bloody legs behind. The half-breed would have none of that; he pulled out his thirteen-inch bowie knife, walked over and buried it to the hilt in the man's back, piercing the heart and stopping all movement.

"The Seminoles are right," said Jebediah, from the back of the room. "He does have a black spirit."

Hunter was on one knee, wiping the blade of his knife on the fat, half man's shirt, and looking around the saloon. The barkeep and the man playing poker had fled. Jebediah and Walt were still seated at their table, cards in their hands, like nothing had happened. The gunslinger grabbed his bottle off the bar and moseyed on over, sitting down across from the old men.

"Are you all up or down?" asked Hunter, as he filled all their glasses with whiskey.

"'Bout even, and that's all we're gonna' be. You done killed or run off all the players from this fine establishment."

"Sorry 'bout that," said Hunter. "Did it ever cross your minds that I coulda used some help?"

"Hell, son," said Jebediah, "there was only three of um."

Walt chimed in, "You know, Hunter James, at our age we find sometimes its best fer us just to stay out of it."

They all slammed back the shots then stood at the same time. "I think it's time to git," said Hunter.

"I'm outta here," said Walt.

"You don't hafta' tell me twice," agreed Jebediah.

The two old men gathered their belongings while Hunter reloaded the shotgun and changed out the Colt's cylinder for full ones. Walt snatched a couple of full bottles from the bar for the long road, sporting a big grin as he did so.

Jebediah and Walt knew where they were headed and they wished the half-breed would come with them, but they knew he had unfinished business and, more importantly, a black heart to feed.

CHAPTER THREE

The gunslinger and the old men rode together for a short time, soon saying their good-byes in a short and not so sweet manner. Men of these times did not live long. Jebediah and Walt were considered lucky for avoiding the six-foot-under rule for so many years.

It just goes to show, only the good die young, the old coots would say, but Hunter knew this saying was false. A lot of bad men died young at his hand, not too long ago. And that was where he was headed, back to Myakka, in search of the one who got away. The old men knew the name of this man, and now, so did he.

Jebediah and Walt were moving to the northeast to hunt black bear near Indian Town, on the east side of Lake Okeechobee. Hunter was heading toward Myakka, northwest on the other side of the lake and far beyond. They all had many days riding ahead of them, and only God new where they would end up.

Mid-summer and hotter than Hades, the sun had set into the glades twice since Hunter said good-bye to the only two people he knew on this Earth. As depressing as that sounds, it was much worse than that. For the first time in almost a year, Hunter allowed himself to think of Lilith, Matt, and the boy.

He sat at a small fire under the stars of a clear, southern night sky. There were no tears or sounds of sadness, there was only the thickness of the air from the need for revenge, once again building up inside of him. A man can keep devastating thoughts from his mind for only so long before he must act. The frog legs he was eating began to sour in his stomach, so with a grimace he threw his supper into the fire, turning to the bottle of whiskey calling to him from inside his saddlebag.

He sat there drinking and staring into the flames, settling him down just a bit. He knew he would finish off most of the bottle after the first sip; not wise being passed out drunk out here in hostile country with a bounty on your head, in the middle of a war. After a while, he began dozing off... in and out... in again... Right now, he didn't give a shit, and that would be his last thought of this night.

He was awakened by the morning sun and Zeke's wet nostrils blowing air on his face. Hunter rolled away, wiping animal snot from his cheek.

"Dammit, horse."

Zeke whinnied, moving his head and neck up and down, followed by a hoof scrape.

Hunter looked around; luckily there were no threats upon him. He got to his feet and rubbed the Appaloosa's long face.

"Good boy. You knew I was in danger, you knew my inner clock was broke. You know what, boy? You're the only one I got left."

Hunter suddenly had an urge to get moving, not to mention a serious urge to piss. The day was wasting away and he had business to attend to in Myakka. After relieving himself, Hunter packed up camp. *What a beautiful day,* he thought, as he headed down the trail.

He hadn't been in the saddle for more than ten minutes when he found himself face to face with twelve Seminole Indian warriors.

The gunslinger's head had a slight bourbon pain to it, but it quickly went away. He was out-numbered, and would only see another day if these red men decided to allow it. The trail was narrow and there was nothing but Cypress trees and swamp all around.

They instantly surrounded him on all sides. He could take out four or five at most, before being killed. He knew he would not leave this place.

The elder and clear leader of this party, with deeply leathered lines in his face and scars of wars of the past, spoke to him in broken English.

"I am Apayaka Hadjo, war chief of the Miccosukee. The blue coats call me Sam Jones. Why you here on our land?"

"This trail is as good as any," replied Hunter. "It's between where I'm comin' from, and where I must go. There is no why."

Hunter and Sam Jones stared into each other's eyes for a moment looking for fear; there was none to be seen. This did not surprise Hunter, but it did surprise the chief, though he did not show it. The gunslinger knew this game they were playing very well; it was like poker, the problem was no one here was bluffing.

"You have red blood," said Apayaka, this was a statement not a question.

"My mother was lower Creek, my father an outlaw."

"Yes, half-breed, what they call *bastard;* this will not save you," said Sam Jones.

"No," said Hunter. "My blood won't save me, but my destiny will, for my black heart speaks to me so." A warrior to Hunter's left spoke to the chief in their native tongue.

The gunslinger understood the language from his childhood but he did not let on, because now was the time for bluffing.

"*Lus-tee Manito Nak-nee?*" said the chief. "What is your Christian name?"

Hunter suddenly felt a twinge of hope that he might just get out of this unlucky predicament. "Hunter James Dolin."

"I have heard of this. You bad medicine, James Dolin," said the chief. "You may go; my people have suffered much, bad magic we do not want. If we kill you, bad spirit will release over our lands – this cannot be."

"I reckin not," replied Hunter, as he tipped his hat to the Chief, immediately pushing the Appaloosa forward before they changed their minds.

The Indians moved aside reluctantly, allowing him to pass.

The gunslinger rode on down the trail without looking back, leaving the brave but superstitious warriors behind.

CHAPTER FOUR

Scooter Johnson was a convincing man, he'd had lots of practice over the years for he had been a scoundrel and a liar all his life. He had convinced the Army that a small band of Indians, led by a half-breed named Hunter James Dolin, had committed atrocities against the Myakka City and the state of Florida. He claimed they murdered the white ranchers and burned the town to the ground. Since there was no one left alive to dispute his claims, this was an easy sell.

For his fortitude, he was rewarded land in Myakka, the very same plot of land where Matt's saloon once stood. Scooter had rebuilt the hotel and saloon damn near exactly as it was before. A well-stocked trading post was also rebuilt across the dirt road, by the same man that had occupied it before; his name was Chuck Lamb. He had known Matt for a long time, and he knew the truth of what had happened to the city a little over one year ago.

But Chuck was a survivor and he knew when to keep his mouth shut. That's why he was still alive and once again back in business at the ripe old age of fifty-two. He did not like the new owner of Matt's saloon, but business was business, and he had goods for sale to anyone who had the coin to buy. If he only sold to good men that he liked, he would damn near have zero customers.

Chuck Lamb was no fool and Scooter Johnson wasn't a fool either. He had five gunmen under his hire for one purpose and one purpose only, to protect him and his establishment from a vengeful savage. He had feared from day one that the half-breed would seek him out and kill him, or worse. But as time went on, Scooter became more comfortable in his surroundings, even though he had not heard any news of Hunter's capture or killing. The blue coats had left Florida to fight the Bushwhackers up in east Tennessee and northern Virginia. Scooter figured with all that was going on there was more than a good chance the half-breed was dead or gone.

While Myakka City was up and running again, and the past basked in the glow of forgotten denial, a rider and his Appaloosa horse was coming, bringing with him the rain.

◆❖◆

The storm hit hard at first, as lightning lit up the dark sky followed by claps of thunder. The wind finally stopped blowing the rain sideways and the drops were now coming straight down, light but steady. Hunter wore the long coat he kept buried in his saddlebags during the dry weather. The coat was made of buffalo leather and waterproofed with oil from the animal that was melted down from its fat; this kept the gunslinger's weapons dry as the coat went down to the tops of his boots. The last thing he wanted was wet powder causing a misfire in the middle of a gun battle. Something as simple as the luxury of a rain-shedding coat was as important to a fighting man as the guns he carried.

With the rain steadily dripping from the brim of his hat, Hunter dismounted in front of Scooter's saloon tethering Zeke to the hitching post. He stopped and stared at that wood post for a moment, recognizing it even in the darkness. Plainly, it had survived the fire of Myakka. He then looked to the front porch, remembering Matt; many times, they sat there drinking and talking through the smoke of their cigars.

At his right were three other horses hitched beside him. One of them blew air from its nose, getting Hunter's attention and directing his gaze to the north. There, in the shadows, was a partial staircase left from the very barn where his old friend Matt had died. It also reminded him of the stable boy, Zeke, who he met right here on this very ground, for the first time.

His anger grew as he pushed all thoughts of Lilith, the only woman he had ever loved, from creeping into his mind. Hunter walked up the three steps onto the porch. Now that he was under the roof and out of the rain; he removed his trench coat and hung it on a nail that was jutting out from the building. He pulled the double-barrel sawed-off shotgun from his side-shoulder holster, breaking it and checking the shells for moisture. Satisfied, he flicked his arm in an upward motion, snapping it shut. With the barrels facing forward and held firmly in both hands, the gunslinger entered the saloon through the swinging doors.

The sound of the constant downpour of the rain concealed any noise of his entrance into the drinking establishment. He stood just inside the doorway looking around quickly with his eyes, barely moving his head. His steel blue eyes took in the room and every man in it. There was a tall skinny man behind the bar and two roughnecks at the counter, drinking with their backs to him.

He saw that they had quick-draw holsters, which gave away their profession without their admission. There were three more men playing cards at a back table; they were the only ones safe from the scatter-gun, due to their distance.

The bartender, the first to spot the gunslinger, immediately looked terrified.

"By the look on your face, you must be Scooter," stated Hunter.

The two men at the bar turned, their hands going to the butts of their guns in chorus. What they saw standing before them was a tall man with long jet-black hair, wearing a hat that matched it perfectly, raindrops dripping from its brim. He was holding a shotgun with the two large barrel holes aimed right at them, no more than ten paces away.

"Easy simmer," said Hunter.

"Who the devil er' you?" asked the man closest to him.

"No, no," replied Hunter. "The question is, who the devil do you want to continue to be?"

At that moment, the three men at the back table stood, their chairs sliding on the floor in unison as they pulled their guns and started moving forward.

The talk was over; Hunter pulled both triggers of the shortened 12-gauge, blasting the two gunfighters, and opening up their bellies as they were too late on the draw.

Scooter hit the floor behind the bar.

Hunter dropped the sawed-off, pulled his 44 Colts, and began firing at the men approaching from the back of the saloon. The three were fanned out and firing, but they were hesitant and more concerned with being shot than shooting.

This was where the half-breed gunslinger always had an advantage. He stood steadfast, not caring if he lived or if he died. He had no weak nerve to contend with; he just fired while aiming true and pulling the triggers. The gunslinger drew both pistols simultaneously with the speed of a rattlesnake strike. He shot the man to his left in the chest with his left-hand Colt. At the same time, the man to his right made a gurgling sound as the bullet from his right-hand revolver pierced his liver.

Through the smoke, the revolver in his left hand thundered once again as his right moved to the man in the middle. After opening his belly, his right gun shifted back to the man on the right for another hit. His left Colt shot the man on the left once again as he was falling forward, putting a bullet in his left cheek and out the back of his head. Without hesitation, his right Colt fired back to the middle, accompanied by the left, hitting the scoundrel and not wasting a shot.

The following silence seemed more deafening than the previous sound of gunfire, as it always seemed to do. Hunter dropped the depleted cylinders from his pistols and replaced them with new ones from his belt. He was waiting for the smoke to clear and wondering where Scooter might be lurking when he heard shuffling coming from behind the bar.

With his Colts loaded and holstered, he picked up the shotgun from the floor where it had landed. He broke it and removed the empties, then dug two new shells from the sewn in sleeves inside his coat, and slid them into the chambers. With one quick move he flicked his forearm, locking in the barrels to the stock, and pulling back both triggers with his thumb.

Hunter heard another scraping noise moving away from him; this time he was able to pinpoint the sound, coming from behind the bar.

"Scoo-o-tter-r-r-r, I hear you back there," Hunter taunted as he slowly walked toward the other end of the saloon's counter. *Ba-boom, clank, ba-boom, clank* was the sound of his boots and spurs as he walked. Hunter got to the end of the bar and turned at the opening. There on the floor, with a gun in his hand, was Scooter Johnson crawling on his belly like the snake that he was.

The gunslinger crushed the man's hand with a boot until he screamed and released the revolver. "Scooter!" said Hunter. "where do you think you're goin'?"

"Go to hell, you stinkin' Injun bastard."

Hunter pushed down even harder with the heel of his boot, two of Scooter's fingers split out the side, spewing blood onto the dirt floor.

"AAAGGGHHH!" screamed Scooter.

Hunter flipped the shotgun around. "Goodnight, belly snake," he said and hit him in the back of the head with the butt end, knocking him clean out.

◆❖◆

I'm cold, my head hurts, and my hand hurts, thought Scooter. *Where am I? What the hell happened?* Scooter's eyelids felt like lead balls as he continued to try to push them open. After some labored flickering, they finally did just that. The problem he had now was focusing; he could see the ground through the blurriness and felt the cold dirt on his left cheek. After some thought, he realized he was laying on his stomach and his hands were tied behind his back. His ankles were latched together too.

"Hey!" Scooter yelled, but it came out not much louder than a whisper.

"Over here, belly snake."

Scooter blinked his eyes several times trying to focus. As his vision cleared, he could see the gunslinger sitting on a rock and plucking the feathers off of a dead chicken, its neck was dangling, clearly broken.

"What are you doin'?" asked he.

"Oh, I'm feedin' my buddies over in the creek, stirrin' them up just a bit."

Scooter tried to turn his head to look around; he could not see the water but he could hear it behind him. He looked back to Hunter, his head hurting as he did so.

"What the hell are ya talkin' bout? You're crazy." Scooter was getting very nervous, one look at that savage Injun son-of-a-bastard and he knew he was in big trouble, but he wasn't sure what that trouble was.

"No, not crazy," said the gunslinger, "What do you call it, vengeful maybe. You and your friends killed people I cared about, and now you will suffer for that – you're the last, end of story."

"What are you gonna' do?" asked Scooter desperately.

"Well," explained Hunter, "I'm gonna do a little fishin'." Hunter stood from his rock and chucked the dead featherless chicken into the creek.

Scooter could hear thrashing in the water behind him as he struggled nervously to look around.

"Well, let's git on with it," said Hunter, as he grabbed Zeke's reins and started moving the horse forward.

Scooter was dragged backwards by his ankles; panic began to set in as his mind began to register what was happening.

Hunter tapped the Appaloosa on the hindquarters, moving the horse quicker and slinging Scooter upside down – up and out, over the water. Pieces of cut chicken fell down and dangled from rawhide strings, coming to rest two feet below his head.

Scooter was swinging like a pendulum as very large gators came up out of the water and snapped at the chicken, just out of reach of the man's head. Scooter was screaming again, as Hunter backed Zeke up a bit, putting his face and head closer to the teeth-laden jaws of the twelve foot reptiles. The largest of the gators stretched his neck up and snapped two pieces of chicken hanging down less than a foot from Scooter Johnson's head.

"PULL ME UP!!!! PULL ME UP!!!!" shrieked the dangling man.

"I'm not the last – Montgomery's alive! *HE'S ALIVE, PLEASE!!!"*

Hunter urged the Appaloosa forward so the rope hanging over the branch moved with him, pulling Scooter up and out of the reach of the gator's bite.

"What do you mean, *he's alive?"* yelled Hunter. "I blowed him up in his own hotel."

"NO, NO!!!" said Scooter, calming just a bit, "Think about it – did you see him? He sent his men in there, but he stayed behind."

Hunter dug deep into his memories; he'd been in the ravine behind the hotel that he had wired with black powder. He waited to see the men show themselves in the back window before he pushed down the plunger. He could not remember actually seeing Richard Montgomery. The man who shot his Lilith, his one love, in the head execution style.

"Dammit all to hell," Hunter said aloud. "Where's Montgomery now?"

"He built a house on Lake Okeechobee, I don't know wheres. *PLEASE*, let me down, I beg you," pleaded Scooter as he dangled just out of reach of the hungry gators.

"Yeah, I'll let you down," replied Hunter.

"Oh, thank God, thank you, God!" said Scooter, almost crying with relief.

"God's got nothin' to do with it," replied the gunslinger, as he quickly pulled out his Bowie knife and slashed the rope, cutting it a foot from the saddle horn.

Scooter's screams were short as he dropped head first into the hungry jaws of the feeding gators, the large reptiles thrashed furiously as they tore the man apart; 'til there was nothing left but red-colored water and a few short pieces of rope.

Hunter James Dolin packed up his gear, feeling no regrets. This man was a scoundrel, and deserved to die. *Who names a kid Scooter anyhow? Should have named you gator bait,* thought Hunter. He mounted Zeke and got back on his revenge trail, riding southeast with renewed purpose, toward Lake Okeechobee.

CHAPTER FIVE

Richard Montgomery was a wealthy man; he had struck it rich some years back in Colorado, known at the time as the Pikes Peak Gold Rush of 1859. After Montgomery had mined his claims dry, he moved in on other miner's lands with vigor – the men who would not sell outright were run off or murdered. His money bought him many men who had no problem killing for their living. That was where a young sixteen-year-old girl named Lilith Bailer was found in hiding, after her father refused to sell Richard Montgomery his land. When the smoke cleared, he took her for his own. He told everyone she was his daughter, but unfortunately for her, they were much closer than that.

When the War Between the States seemed to be inevitable, Montgomery traveled to Myakka City, Florida, where with his riches he built a hotel way out of the reach of the fighting armies. What he did not plan on was his Lilith falling in love and running off with a half-breed. His men managed to capture Lilith and in an act of retaliation, Montgomery shot her in the head in the presence of her lover, Hunter James Dolin.

This action resulted in the killing of many men and the destruction of the city. Montgomery was a smart man, as well as unconscionable, and in the end he sent his men into the gunslinger's trap and watched from a safe distance as his hotel exploded. He searched all around for any survivors. Richard assumed the half-breed was killed in the explosion along with his men, so he mounted his horse and left the town behind, leaving it to burn.

Unknown to Montgomery, Hunter had escaped out the back of the building finding refuge in the ravine where his plunger awaited. The gunslinger had dug himself from under the debris to find no one left alive. He presumed Montgomery was dead, and moved on.

It took Richard Montgomery a little over a year to build a new army of men, along with a mansion on the north side of Lake Okeechobee. The southern style home was like no other anywhere in the state of Florida, or any other place on record. Stilted, it stood ten feet off the ground with three floors above that. The first floor had four bedrooms on the four corners of the rectangular shaped building. Located in the center of the floor plan was a fully equipped kitchen along with the eating area.

The second floor was Richard Montgomery's private space, divided into two rooms: one was a large sitting area equipped with leather-backed chairs; the second was his sleeping quarters fitted with a custom built bed and matching dressers. All the furniture had been shipped in from North Carolina on a steamboat that Montgomery owned. The third and last level had four bedrooms on the four corners like the first, the center of this level had a small living area, mostly consisting of boxes of rifles, boxes of ammunition and boxes of dynamite. All three floors had a single fireplace connected to the same chimney running up the outside of the building. The third floor fireplace was never used due to the dynamite and ammunition stored there.

On top of the flat roof stood a waist-high wood wall that went all the way around, like a crow's nest for riflemen. In the middle of the roof was a trap door that had stairs which ran all the way down to the first floor, allowing access to the top from any part of the house.

There were railed balconies on every floor all the way around the building. The first floor balcony was connected to ten-foot wide steps that went from the front doors to the ground. The window openings were covered with planked wood shutters with cross-shaped slits in them to allow for shooting rifles.

The men who lived in the corner rooms on the first and third floors were the best sharpshooters Montgomery could find. These men were well fed and well paid for their loyalty.

This house was a fortress; built to protect a man who made many enemies over the years by murdering men, women, and children for the sole purpose of enriching himself. Richard Montgomery was greedy and evil, but at the same time, he was also educated and clever. He had engineering skills acquired in his youth while building bridges for the railroad which he used to build this great house. Holes were dug for the wood pilings cut from yellow pine trees that measured twelve inches in diameter. They had been driven ten to fifteen feet in the ground with a large lime rock boulder that was dug from the edge of the lake. The rock would be tied to one end of a long rope which would then be thrown over a large tree branch. The other end was then fastened to an ox that would be backed up, raising the boulder. Then the animal was quickly led forward, dropping the rock on top of the log, again and again, guided by men with tag lines and driving the wood down into the mud.

When the house was complete, Montgomery could see only one weakness in its defense, Being built ten feet off the ground and of wood made it vulnerable to fire. He'd instructed his local, hired builders to dig a shallow pond under the entire house. A trench was then dug from Lake Okeechobee to the pond under the house, filling it with water. The fenced in waterhole was stocked with gators, six big ones. The water eliminated the threat of fire and the gators kept anyone from sneaking in from the bottom. The place was a fortress, plain and simple.

Richard Montgomery stood at the end of his dock, which was connected to the front stairs of the house by a four-foot-wide by one-hundred-foot long walkout. This walkout was over the top of the trench that carried the water to the gator pit underneath the fortified mansion.

Richard was overdressed for this part of the country; the only thing that looked casual about him in this time and place was his guns that hung from his waist belt. The pistols were 1862 silver plated, Navy Colt revolvers, 36 Caliber, they were custom made and monogrammed on the pearl-boned handles; the French script simply read, *Master*.

Montgomery was smoking a very expensive Cuban cigar while he watched out over Lake Okeechobee. It was early morning and the fog was thick rising off the top of the lake. His thoughts of *smoke on the water* were interrupted when he heard hooves stomping the ground behind him. He turned to see two of his men dismount and approach, hurrying up the boarded walk. Montgomery did not like the look on their faces as they reached him.

"What's your purpose, Bodie?" asked Richard, as he blew smoke from his nostrils across his black and grey handlebar mustache. "You're interrupting my quiet time."

"Sorry, Mr. Montgomery, but we have some news from Myakka."

Trenton Bodie was his name. He was six-foot-five, skinny looking, and bowlegged. His shoulders were extra wide, but thin. Strong as an ox, many men had made the mistake of challenging him. He was ex-Army and smarter than most – in fact; he was Richard's right-hand man.

"Well?" insisted Montgomery. "You know I'm not a very patient man."

"Yes sir... We were headin' back from that thing you sent us to do."

"Did you take care of it?" interrupted Richard.

"Yes sir, he won't be testifyin', never."

"Good, good. Have the chink cook you all up a steak, and some whiskey too."

"Thank ya, Mr. Montgomery." Bodie turned to the young man to his right. "Birdie, git on up to the house and start that Chinaman on them beef steaks. I'll be there, right shortly."

"Yes sir, Bode." The tall and skinny blonde boy, with the hooknose that looked like a beak, turned on his heel and ran back up the wood walk.

Richard spoke, bringing Bodie's attention back to him, "By the look on your face and the way you shooed that boy away, I'd say you have somethin' else on your mind."

"There's more news from Myakka, sir, and it ain't none too good."

Richard could see the concern on his face; he knew from experience that Trenton Bodie feared no man. Montgomery suddenly had a bad feeling that ran up his spine and tightened the back of his neck.

"Well, spill it, Bodie – what you got?"

"Like I says, me and Birdie were headed back from takin' care of that business when we took a mind to stop at Scooter's to git a drink. We found Scooter's men dead, shot full of holes. By the size of um, I'd say 44s. They were precision shots, boss."

Montgomery began rubbing the back of his neck as it tightened even more.

Bodie continued after a slight pause. "There were two others, bounty hunters. Their guts were spilled, buckshot by the looks – I'd say sawed-off."

"Son-of-a-bitch!" involuntarily escaped Montgomery's lips. "What about Scooter?"

"He was missin'; we found a blood trail dragged out the back door."

"Did you foller it?" asked Richard.

"Yes sir; it led us to a water hole, gator filled. There was shredded clothin' and some chewed up pieces of rope. Looked like he were dangled over um like a side of beef, before he was dropped."

"How do you know he was dropped, Bodie?"

"Birdie boy found a boot, with a foot and part of a shin bone in 'er."

"*Shit!*" exclaimed Richard. "You know that lily-livered..." As soon as he said the word *lily*, the reality of what was coming hit Richard like a sledge hammer. "Scooter talked – that means he's comin' for me."

"It's him, ain't it. The half-breed..." This was more a statement than a question from Bodie.

Montgomery did not answer. Instead, he ordered, "We got men strewn all over; send the word and git them back here right quick. But don't mention a word about the half-breed, or some of them won't show, got it?"

"Yes sir, boss, right quick," agreed Bodie, as he headed toward the house for that steak. The boy named Birdie would have to get his to go, for he had to round up the men for the trouble that was surely on its way.

Richard Montgomery turned back to the lake; *Where is she?* he thought. *She's a day late. I could really use her now, 'cause I got to kill that savage gunslinger once and for all.* He left the dock for the house, knowing there was much to prepare. The gunslinger was coming, and death would surely follow.

Chapter Six

Jebediah and Walt were hunting black bear on the southeast side of Lake Okeechobee, where they found some tracks early on. They had been following them for a week now, and these prints were the biggest either man had ever seen in these parts. Both of them had an idea what they had here, but neither was willing to admit it out loud.

Until Walt spoke up. He just couldn't hold his silence any longer. "Jebediah, you ain't said a word in three days, I know'd you as long as I can remember; are you thinkin' what I'm thinkin'?"

Jebediah was leading the way, as always. Not because he was a better tracker than Walt, but because his eyesight had not left him just yet. He replied over his shoulder without stopping, "What you tryin' to say, Walt?"

"Well, you know as well as I do this ain't no black bear we're follerin'. From the size and depth of them there tracks, we're talkin', twelve maybe fifteen hundred pounds. Ain't no blackies git that big."

Walt rode alongside Jebediah, the paw prints in between their horses run south through the muddy trail.

"I didn't want to say nothin', 'til I seen *IT*," said Jebediah. "But you're right, we got us a brown bear – maybe even a grizz." Walt pulled back on the reins, bringing his black and grey Cracker horse to a halt.

Jebediah did the same, his Cracker horse was colored chestnut and slightly larger.

They looked eye to eye for the first time in a while; the reason being the ground required their full attention when tracking game from horseback. They both felt stiffness in their necks from the change of position.

Walt massaged his neck as he replied in bewilderment, "I ain't never heard of a grizzly travelin' any wheres near this far south. I heard a' one shot in the Carolinas once, but that were clear up in the Smokies."

"Yeah, I hear yah," said Jebediah. He took advantage of their stop to light up a cigar. "I been thinkin' bout it, and the only thing I can figure is them battles between the North and South has run this bad boy deep in the wrong direction."

Walt nodded his head in agreement. "That makes sense, Jebediah. I did take to mind these tracks are squirrelly, like this bear is lost and not sure where he wants to go."

"All righty then. Let's git 'im, Walt. Hell, we'll be famous."

"Yeah, or we'll be dead."

They both chuckled a bit while they moved on.

An hour or so had gone by when the trail was lost at the edge of the black water of a still-water swamp, where the bear tracks simply stopped. The old men dismounted, their snow-white hair blowing in the steady breeze. Jebediah walked along the edge of the water one way, while Walt walked it on the other. They both stood with their hands on their hips, staring into the Cypress swamp.

"Shit! Can you believe it?" exclaimed Walt.

"Yup, that crazy bear went straight through the bog." said Jebediah as he walked over to Walt's side. "We can foller, but that water's knee high, at the least."

"To hell with the water," replied Walt. "I ain't goin' through that." He pointed with his crooked index finger at the black fog about twenty feet into the swamp. As bad as Walt's vision was, he could still see that the fog was moving.

"Skeeters," said Jebediah.

"Yup, skeeters," answered Walt, "Not to mention gittin' eatin' alive, they're so thick we'd choke on 'em." At that moment, Walt slapped at his ear, as a mosquito buzzed in it.

"Well, we could ride south around the edge," suggested Jebediah, "and try to head him off on the other side."

"That sounds like a good i-dear, Jebediah, We can pick up his exit trail, or if we git there first, we can wait 'im out."

"We better git movin' then, Walt." Jebediah nodded in the direction of the black fog of mosquitoes slowly coming at them; the swarm now only about ten feet from the edge of the marsh.

"They smell us, all right," said Walt, as they both quickly mounted their horses and spurred them to a run, riding south along the outskirts of the black-water swamp, glad to leave the bugs behind.

They traveled miles without stopping, until an hour before sundown. They would set up camp for the night and both agreed they should sleep in shifts. These seasoned hunters knew that within a blink of an eye they could become the hunted.

◆❖◆

Ten settings of the sun had passed since Hunter James Dolin had ridden away from the gator pit. The gunslinger fondly liked to think of the pit as Scooter's gator soup. Hunter thought of how righteous it would be to get Richard Montgomery in that position, dangling by his ankles over a pool of hungry swamp dragons. Or, better yet, a nest of cottonmouths, for the water moccasins venomous bites would be a slower death and torturous. These thoughts pleased Hunter, but more importantly, they occupied his thoughts – a diversion keeping him from thinking of Lilith and Zeke. He allowed himself to think of Matt more often. Matt was an old man and had lived a long life, died an honorable death – a warrior's death. Lilith was young and innocent, and he had not been able to save her as he'd promised. Zeke was a young boy, born to a hard life in rough times; the gunslinger was unable to save him as well. He had never promised him directly, but he felt the boy expected it, whether the youngster knew it or not.

Revenge became the fuel to the fire that burned inside the gunslinger, keeping him alive with purpose and moving him forward. God willing, he swore he would have his vengeance in this life, or the next. No – he would not be satisfied with the next life, it must be this life, and he would not stop until he was very old or dead.

With these thoughts driving him, Hunter traveled the most direct route possible from the outskirts of Myakka City straight for Lake Okeechobee. His plan was to ride the north rim of the lake until he ran across Montgomery's place, or until he found someone who knew of its where abouts. He had ridden hundreds of miles, stopping only twice in small towns for supplies, all without incident.

In the late afternoon, he sensed a change in the air; it was a smell he knew well. He guided the Appaloosa off the path, maneuvering through a patch of yellow pines, breaking out onto the shore of the giant lake, Lake Okeechobee; which in the native language means *Big Water*. There wasn't a lake in the state that came close to its equal.

The half-breed looked out over the fresh-water sea as a steady breeze attempted to blow his black-brimmed hat from his head. The air was warm, fresh, and clean. He decided to settle in for the day.

Dismounting, he walked Zeke back into the pine forest and tethered him to a tree. He pulled a hatchet from a loop on his saddle, and walked deeper into the thickest part of the woods where he chopped down five small pines to make a clearing. He took the cut trees and turned them horizontally to form a wall by tying them to live trees with rawhide. There were two reasons for this wall; one, to block the wind from the lake and the other was to shield the light of the fire from being seen. He raked up leaves and sediment with a branch he had cut. Hunter stacked some dead twigs into a tepee shape and stuffed it with Spanish moss, then leaned bigger dead wood over that, forming the same shape. Removing the steel tip from one of his arrows, he quickly spun the shaft between his palms, the wood tip pressing on a split branch of a palm frond. The friction created heat, catching the moss he dropped on top of it. This happened easily for the ground was dry due to lack of rain.

With a small but potent fire going, Hunter fetched Zeke and walked him to the clearing. The half-breed's stomach was growling at him as he removed the app's saddle for the night. The sun was dropping in the sky, but he still had time left before full dark. Hunter grabbed his bow and a tipped arrow, along with a pre-cut length of twine from his saddlebag and made his way through the trees to the edge of the lake.

On the way, he picked up a four-foot long by two-inch diameter branch from the edge of the woods and pushed it down into the mud, like a skinny fence post at the water's edge. He then tied one end of the twine to the back end of his arrow and the other end he tied at the top of the vertical stick. He set the bow and arrow down on the bank and began digging through the wet soil. The worms were many; as they wiggled in his hands in an attempt to escape, he chucked them into the water a good twenty feet from shore.

Within seconds, the Crappie were thrashing as they fed on their wiggly meal. The bow-slinger brushed the black sand from his hands before picking up his bow and arrow and firing it into the frenzy. He snatched up the line tied to the arrow and pulled it toward him, the palm-size fish resisting all the way. Hunter repeated this five more times; throwing more worms into the lake between shots to chum those to the surface until he had three half-pound Crappie, wounded but still flopping further up the shore behind him. If this were the cold season, Hunter would have shot many more for travel, but in the Florida heat of the summer fish spoiled very quickly, so he only killed what he would eat.

After gutting them and scraping the scales from the fish skins, Hunter cooked them over the fire, skewered with the same arrow that killed them. The white tender meat was delicious; he ate every morsel leaving only the heads and the largest of the bones. As the sun set over the lake, Hunter smoked his last cigar of the day. Then he fell asleep on his bedroll with the double-barrel shotgun lying across his mid-section, leaving Zeke as lookout, as was the horse's job so many times before.

Hunter James awoke with the sun and to the calling sounds of an osprey flying high in the morning sky. Ever since the surprise run-in with Sam Jones and his warriors, Hunter slept in full gear, from his guns to his boots. Zeke was another matter; the horse was stripped of his rig nightly, for he was pulling double-duty. Hunter had lost his packhorse months ago when it had come up lame, most likely from hoof rot. It was never a pleasant thing shooting your own horse, but the extra meat was a nice change from gator tails and snake backs.

The first thing Hunter did after waking was to saddle the Appaloosa for travel. He never knew when uninvited company might arrive, especially being a wanted man with a large bounty on his head. With this done, Hunter covered the warm coals of the spent fire with sand; he grabbed his tin cup and filled it a quarter full with salt from his pack. He walked to the edge of the lake and filled the tin with water. He drank, gargled, and swished the salty liquid between his teeth, swallowing some, and spitting out the rest. He was staring into the bottom of the cup wishing he had some coffee grounds for it, when he spotted a flash on the horizon of the ocean-size lake. Hunter stood from his squatting position and put his hand to his brow to block the sun's glare off the water. It was definitely a steamboat; it appeared to be moving north. Hunter moved quickly up the bank, through the trees into the clearing. Zeke whinnied, thrashing his head as he was spooked a bit from the fast movement. "Easy boy," reassured Hunter. "It's time to move on."

He unraveled the reins from the tree branch and slung himself onto the horse's back, maneuvering him through the trees to the edge of the grassy beach. Pulling back on the reins, they came to a halt. Hunter then dug around in one of his saddlebags 'til he found what he was looking for. His sixteen-inch telescope, a gift from the U.S. Army some years back. The safest way to track and kill Indians is from a distance, so it's quite an advantage if you spot them before they spot you.

Hunter extended the spyglass to its full length, and then putting it up to one eye while closing the other, he began scanning the horizon for the boat. He had seen paddle steamers on the lake several times, but he had never seen one like this before. This one was a steam ship; much larger than most military vessels that traveled these waters. The large red paddlewheel was located at the stern and an oversize drop-gate was at the bow for reaching a landing place easier in the shallows. The tall smoke stacks were mid-ship, one port, one starboard.

There were two Gatling guns on platforms – one was near the stern and the other was mounted on the bow. They appeared to be on swivels; Hunter had seen versions of these guns on military vessels but had never seen them on a private ship like this one. As he panned the ship with the scope, he counted five men on deck, all armed with rifles and side arms, none wore uniforms in blue or grey. These men were not military, and the hundred and seventy-foot steamer flew no flags.

While Lee and Grant fought over lands in South Carolina and Tennessee, other men in leadership saw the advantages of playing the middle for power and profit. Like the Comanchero's of the west, they bought and sold guns to the white armies as well as the Indians. These kinds of men had no honor to God and Country; they were driven only by greed.

The ship looked to be at full speed, and was almost out of spyglass range when Hunter caught a glimpse of the steamboat's name.

With his teeth clenched near the breaking point, the gunslinger cursed, *"SON-OF-A-BITCH!!!!"* He immediately knew who owned this battleship and where it was heading.

"He named it after *her*," said Hunter under his breath. "I can't believe he named it after her." With heat rising in his throat, the half-breed gunslinger put the telescope away. "YAH!" he yelled as he spurred the Appaloosa to a run, riding north with one thought on his mind – the torture and death of one Richard Montgomery.

Chapter Seven

Walt woke up at four a.m. like clockwork. With sleep-filled eyes he saw that Jebediah was already up drinking coffee. Jebidiah had the last shift on the bear watch, one sleeping and one at the watch; but regardless of their cautious schedule, they always woke at four a.m. The older they got the less sleep they seemed to need.

Walt would say, "I'm gittin' old and runnin' outta days. I'll git plenty of time to sleep when I'm dead."

Jebediah would shake his head in agreement and pronounce, "It's called a dirt nap, Walt. We'll git plenty of rest then, won't we?" Laughter would immediately follow, usually accompanied with a shot of whiskey, but not this morning.

Lately it had been more coffee and less hooch, for they were on a bear hunt. And this wasn't any ordinary bear; this was a Kodiak or a grizzly. These old coots had been hunting bear all their lives and they had never heard of a brown bear traveling this far south, ever. They were under the assumption that this bear was crazed, a rogue that was twelve-hundred pounds of danger equipped with teeth and claws powered by its brute strength.

"What do you think, Jebediah?" asked Walt as they packed up camp for travel. "We been half-way 'round this here bog swamp, and there ain't no sign to be found."

"I hear yah," replied Jebediah, as he kicked dirt on what was left of their camp fire. "He's a sly son-of-a-gun. I figure as I think on it, he turned around at some point and went out the way he'd come, or, he turned west and went out the side somewheres."

Walt mounted his steed, as did Jebediah. "You're figurin' sounds right, Jebediah. We'll ride west around the rim, and then north the way we come from, try to pick up some tracks. Hell, maybe that critter's lying in the middle of that black-water swamp, dead with distemper."

"I half-hope you're right, Walt. I'm not sure I want to find this bear. The way my bones were aching this mornin', I just might be gittin' too old for this shit."

The old men both chuckled aloud as they turned their Cracker horses to the west, leaving the sun to rise at their backs. At a steady walk, they moved around the edge of the swamp with their heads down, looking for tracks of a beast that neither man was sure he wanted to find.

The old boys rode all day, stopping only to relieve themselves and pull jerky from their packs; they ate, smoked, and drank water from the saddle. It was late afternoon and neither man had touched their whiskey bottles, which was unfamiliar territory for these two men. The earlier they started the day, the earlier they felt like drinking, and as always the old men awoke before the sun. But today was different, this day they were hunting a devil. With age comes wisdom and they knew they would have to be at their best if they wanted to come out of this hunting expedition alive.

Jebediah was leading the way a good ten feet above the swampy tree line. Walt was four horse lengths behind him and twenty feet or so up from that same line. This was a standard formation they used to cover more territory. They were approximately twenty miles from where the bear tracks had first entered the swamp days ago, almost creating a giant circle, when

Jebediah came to a halt. He immediately pulled his Henry rifle from its saddle-sheath and cocked the lever action, loading a .50 caliber cartridge.

Walt was looking down for signs when he was alerted by the cocking sound of Jeb's rifle. Walt pulled his eight gauge, double long barrel shotgun and thumb pulled both hammers back.

"What is it, Jebediah?" asked Walt in a whisper.

"He came out here, Walt," also in a whisper, "and the tracks route into that saw-grass over yonder; the footpaths are fresh."

Jeb's rifle pointed toward a large field of grass thirty feet from the swampy forest edge which didn't give them a whole lot of room if that bear decided to charge out at them from the hedge of sharp-sided foliage.

"Dammit Jeb, he's gone from skeeter infested swamp to saw-grass, that greenery is horse neck high; it'll cut us up fer sure."

"*SHUSH...* I hear somthin' movin'," pleaded Jebediah.

There was a slight shuffling sound coming from the tall grass patch, Jebediah's horse became uneasy, perhaps sensing danger. The wind was blowing at their backs, putting them upwind of whatever was lurking in the brush. The bear could smell them while leaving Walt, Jebediah, and their mounts guessing.

"Easy boy," said Jebediah, as he stroked the horse's neck.

"Hey partner," warned Walt. "I got a bad feelin'..."

Just at that moment the bear charged at Jebediah from the grass. His chestnut Cracker horse reared up on its hind legs in a panic with a loud whinny. The huge grizzly did the same, standing on his back legs while letting out a vicious growl. The height of the horse's muzzle was at the bear's chest as the bear was that much taller. They looked to be preparing for some crazy dance – the horse's hooves and the bear's claw-ridden paws were less than two feet apart.

Jebediah was hanging on for dear life, one hand on the reins and the other clutching his rifle. Jeb was in a compromising position, leaving him unable to get off a shot.

That's when Walt went into action; while trying to settle down his animal he dared not let go of the reins, but he somehow managed to firmly grasp both hands around his eight gauge. Pulling both the triggers, he fired the double barrel shotgun from his hip. Both slugs hit the twelve hundred pound bear in the side. Walt didn't see if he hit the target, for when the loud bang of that shotgun went off, his horse reared up, throwing him off backwards to the ground.

Jebediah wasn't doing much better. When the slugs hit the bear, it dropped down onto all fours, pushing Jeb's horse backward past the edge of the swamp water, knocking Jeb off his mount. Water splashed all around him as he landed butt first and legs out stretched. His horse took off at a run, following behind Walt's horse that had already made his hasty retreat from the battle.

Walt was rolling around on the ground trying to get to his feet, unintentionally leaving Jebediah to fend for himself. The giant grizzly was now wounded and totally enraged. Teeth bared, the bear lunged towards Jebediah...

Evidently, the Lord still watched over this man and gifted him the precious seconds he needed to save his skin. From his sitting position and the depths of the black-swamp water up to his waist, Jebediah aimed quickly...

"Bang...chick, chick, bang...chick, chick, bang..." the cracking sound of the rifle echoed through the swamp. Two of the bullets hit the beast in the chest, the third one entered his left eye then exited out the back of his thick skull. The bear was dead when his large snout landed in Jeb's breadbasket, hard enough to knock out all his wind.

He grabbed a hold of that bear's big old head, attempting to keep himself upright in fear of snapping backward and possibly drowning. Jebediah could do nothing but sit there and struggle, that bear's head face down in his lap. He was breathing hard from the weight and trying to catch his breath, when he heard a familiar voice.

"If you two wants to be alone, just say so."

Jebediah looked up to see Walt standing there with the eight gauge cradled in his arms, wearing a big ole grin on his face stretched from ear to ear.

"Git this gol-dang bear off me," attempted Jeb with a yell, "before I suffocates down here."

Walt set his shotgun down and sloshed around to Jebediah's back, grabbing him under each under pit.

"Boy, I wish one of them there plate photo-tog-rifer's was about," Walt grunted as he struggled to slide his partner out from under the weight of the grizzly, "'cause nobody's gonna' believe this shit."

"Shut up and pull, you old coot," begged Jebediah breathlessly.

They managed to get out of the bog and up onto the bank. Jebediah laid down on the grassy terrain, trying to catch his breath.

"You all right?" asked Walt, still unable to wipe the smile from his face.

"Yeah, I'm all right," said Jebediah.

Walt threw him his soaked hat. "You take all the time you need, Jeb, then git a fire started. We got a lot of butcherin' and skinnin' to do. I need to go fetch them lily-livered animals of ours."

"Mine will be close by," assured Jeb. "That black and grey of yours, I ain't too sure about." Jebediah evidentially found his breath along with his sense-of-humor, and he broke out in laughter.

"I guess you'll be all right then, smart-ass," said Walt, while trying not to laugh.

It didn't take too long for Walt to round up their horses, but Jebediah was right, his black and grey was a lot further away than Jeb's chestnut Cracker horse. There was no way Walt was about to mention or admit this ever, come hell or high water.

The old hunters spent the remainder of the after-noon and evening skinning and butchering the great bear. They split the meat evenly between them; they cooked and ate the innards as they worked and packed the rest in salt for preserving. The fur would bring big money, which they would sell to an outpost along the way and, as always, they would divide the payment right down the middle. These two old-timers were brothers in every which ways but blood; they drank whiskey and smoked cigars in celebration late into the night.

With that grizzly carved up and packed away, and not one bit going to waste, Walt and Jebediah slept soundly for the first time in a week, with little worry of being mauled or devoured in their sleep.

CHAPTER EIGHT

Birdie rode hard and fast, rounding up Montgomery's men who were spread out around the countryside. He was instructed to only find the men within a day's ride, order them to drop what they were doing as soon as possible, and return to the home front. The home front was what they all called Richard Montgomery's big house.

The skinny young man called Birdie returned late the night before, slept a good four hours, and now found himself at Bodie's side on the third floor of the large home. Barely eighteen, he did not always see the big picture. "I don't git what all the fuss is about. What can one pissed off half-Injun man do, anyhow?" squawked Birdie. It wasn't just his beak-nose that earned him his nickname, but also his voice – a high-pitched, crow-like sound.

"You did like I told yah, right?" asked Bodie, "You didn't tell the boys why they were being called back to the home front, did yah?"

"I didn't tell no one nothin'. They asked me, I told them the boss talked to Bodie and Bodie told me to round y'all up, that's all I know."

"Good, Birdie," said Bodie, as he patted the boy on the head, "that's a good, Birdie."

"Oh, come on, Bode," said the boy as he jerked his head away in annoyance. "I don't see what the big deal is, anyhow. One half-breed against twenty of us, he's as good as dead, the way I see it."

"Did your bird brain already forgit the bodies in Myakka and what was left of Scooter Johnson in the gator pit?" Bodie asked, as he walked across the room of the third floor. They'd been pulling rifles from crates and checking ammunition for the last hour, at Richard Montgomery's order.

"Well, hell yeah, I remember. I'll never fergit that boot with the foot left in 'er, and that shinbone stickin' outta the top. But Scooter was lily-livered; Mr. Montgomery's men are the meanest I've ever seen."

Bodie was doing inventory on the new Henry repeaters, and checking the action for defects. His mother had been a teacher when he was a boy, so he was one of the few men around who could put pen to paper.

"Boy, you just need to remember two things," said Bodie, raising his voice at the younger. "This man is more deadly than a cornered rattler and twice as fast, and when he comes, you stay close to me. That's an order, you got that?"

The boy was a little surprised by Bodie's outburst. He was a man that never raised his voice. "Yeah, sure, Bode, whatever you say."

"Good," said Bodie, back to his normal tone. "Let's git this work done, and I'll buy you a drink to whet your breakfast appetite."

"Yes sir," Birdie answered. "I ain't had a drink in two days. I was feelin' like my tongue was beginin' to swell." He then made a smacking noise with his mouth, looking even younger than his years to Bodie, for just a moment.

"Well, all right then," said Bodie with a grin.

They worked together in silence, both men feeling good about themselves. Bodie feeling like a concerned father and Birdie feeling like a young man someone might just care about.

The *she* Montgomery was waiting for at the dock was the same battleship Hunter had seen on the big water. The name on the steamboat read, *THE MISS*

LILLY. Richard Montgomery would say he loved the young girl he had imprisoned for his own, the same girl he had shot in the head for her disloyalty to him. Richard was a smart man, but he confused love with infatuation. There was a huge difference between the two that he could not, and never would, understand, It was not in him, not who he was.

Hunter had only known love for a very short time, that feeling now replaced with hate and revenge. This was something Richard Montgomery understood very well.

Richard was out on the dock this morning, smoking a cigar and sipping on a tin cup filled with whiskey. The fog coming off the lake was very thick, visibility near zero.

Since Richard had heard the news of Hunter James Dolin's survival, and the savage's sinister torture of Scooter Johnson in the gator pit, his appetite had been weak. The sour feeling in his stomach was not fear or even nervousness, but more like anticipation. He could not believe that this ghost of a man was still haunting him. After all, he was Richard Montgomery, soon to be the most powerful man in the South. His plans were to fall on the right side of the war, the Union could triumph or the Confederacy, it did not matter which. What mattered to him was the states would be weak and broken in the end and, with his political ties up North, Florida would be his.

Richard stood on the dock, thinking of how wonderful it would be when he became king. He heard a bell *ding,* the sound barely reaching his ears through the fog. He immediately felt excitement in his chest as he quickly walked over to the other end of the twenty-foot dock. There were bollard pilings five feet above the deck for the docking of boats; the one on the end having a large torch wedged in a hole on the top. Richard threw what was left of his whiskey, soaking it. He then took a match from his pocket and, all in one motion, struck it on the back of his pant leg and touched it to the torch. The fire came alive with a flash. Ten seconds went by before the bell began to ring in a signaling fashion: *one, two, three, pause; one, two, three, pause; one, two, three.*

THE MISS LILLY had found her way home. Richard couldn't see the steamer as of yet, but they could see the lit torch mounted on the dock piling, as the bell told. A minute passed; Montgomery could now hear the huge paddle swishing the water to its will. It started as a black shadowy mass as it busted through the fog twenty feet off the dock; the steamship looked like a sea monster as she became visible. The ship bumped into the dock, forcing Richard to take several steps backward and two steps forward to maintain his balance.

A tall thin man with a foot-long, salt and pepper beard walked out the doorway onto the deck of the ship, dressed all in dark blue. His sailor's hat was the same color of black as the eye patch that covered his left eye. Tucked into his black belt was a single Colt Navy revolver, hanging from his right shoulder with a leather strap was a wood stock attachment which could be quickly connected to the pistol for distance shooting.

"Land ho!" yelled the Captain, and he pulled the pin that held up the ramp, located at the center bow of the railing. The heavy wood ramp slammed onto the dock with a bang, two feet from Richard Montgomery's silver tipped, leather boots.

The Captain walked straight down the ramp, stopping a foot from Richard – they locked for a moment in a three-eyed staring contest.

"Monty!" said the captain, with a big smile, showing off his yellow and brown, jagged teeth. "Still same as ever, I see."

"That's right, Captain. It's good you remember what a pain in the ass I can be." They both broke out with laughter as they shook hands, seeming to be two old friends reunited at last. Good news for them, bad news for anyone who would oppose them.

"You're late," said Richard.

"Yeah, I'm late, 'bout a week I expects. In case you didn't know, there's a war goin' on out there."

"I'm not concerned with that for the moment, we got a local problem a brewin' right here."

"What's goin' on?" asked the captain.

"We'll talk on that later," said Richard. "Where is she?"

"I got her locked down. Do you know what two months at sea does to a man?"

Richard was suddenly irritated. "You made my wife a prisoner on my own ship?"

"Easy Monty, it was for her protection. I got ten drunkin' cowboys on this boat, I damn near had a mutiny on my hands."

"Captain," Richard said sternly, "You will refer to me as Mr. Montgomery in front of the men, you got that?"

The Captain took a step back from Richard.

Richard put his hand on his revolver as they resumed their staring contest from earlier.

"So that's how it's gonna' be, then? All right, Monty, this is your show for now."

"Bring her to me, *please*, Captain." This came off as a polite order from Richard.

The Captain pulled a skeleton key from around his neck and then waved it at Richard as he turned and walked up the ramp, disappearing through the doorway.

CHAPTER NINE

The half-breed gunslinger had traveled north to the top of the lake, and then turned west for two days. He was now heading south and following along the shoreline of the big lake. Approaching noon, the fog was finally dissipating as the sun attempted to force its way through the cloudy morn.

Before Scooter Johnson dropped into the gator pit, he told the gunslinger about Montgomery's house located on the north side of Lake Okeechobee. Hunter could travel south for days and still be on the north side of the lake. The temperature was in the nineties, and the humidity was at full throttle; the good news, the overcast continued to block the potent rays of the Florida sun.

Hunter was chewing on a piece of deer jerky and watching an Osprey fly by with a river mullet in its talons when he heard horses moving fast from behind him. He maneuvered the Appaloosa off the shoreline and hastily headed for a small clump of cabbage palms. This was a bad area of the lake to be caught in. The thickness of the woods was a good half-mile to the west, leaving nothing but knee high grass and palm meadow bushes. His only choice was the spread out cluster of palm trees, he decided as he steered Zeke toward it at a dead run. Hunter jumped down from his horse when he reached the backside of the refuge and pulled his rifle from the saddle-sheath. After cocking it slow and as quiet as possible, he aimed it in the direction of the coming riders, steadying it over Zeke's back.

Five men, running strong, passed him by speedily. Had the riders looked toward the trees, they would have spotted the half-breed and his horse; but they were moving too fast for their peripheral vision to catch up, clearly heading for their destination with a purpose.

Hunter leaned his Henry rifle against one of the cabbage palms and dug out his spyglass from his leather saddlebag. Putting it to his eye, he focused on the diminishing horsemen. They were certainly hired guns; the two leaders in his circular view had whips on their saddles, an indication they were Crackers, once running cattle. The other three that followed were sure as hell Missouri Yankees. Hunter knew this from the red leather they wore around their boots. These men were known as *Red Legs*, they were murderers, pure and simple – bands of Union soldiers formed to hunt down and kill rebel guerillas, which led to raping, pillaging, and burning down southern family homes. *What were these Red Legs doin' down this far south in the Florida swamps?* thought Hunter. *Unless they were workin' for Montgomery...*

The gunslinger put away the spyglass and grabbed his rifle from its resting spot against the palm tree before climbing onto Zeke's back. He slid the Henry rifle in its saddle-sheath as he spurred the Appaloosa to a run, in the direction of the horsemen.

Hunter followed the men, careful to keep a safe distance, stopping every once and a while to get a closer look with the telescope. They had slowed their horses to a walk for their much needed rest, so Hunter did the same, shadowing them at every turn. In their arrogance, they did not attempt to cover their trail, making them easy to track. Nightfall was driving the men inland towards the cover of the woods.

Hunter would let the men set up their campsite for the night before he set up his own, picking a strategic location and then deciding on his next move. The half-breed would not strike a fire this evening for the light could reveal his presence. His dinner would be deer jerky and water from his leather pouch and Zeke would have to settle for swamp grass for his nourishment, his supply of grain all but gone.

Hunter made sure they were upwind from the Red Legs' camp; at this distance, their horses' sense of smell would alert them of his presence. The gunslinger pulled the brim of his hat down over his eyes, knowing he only had precious minutes to rest. Time went by quickly; he was compelled to view the sun sink into the lake, bringing on the night. Hunter never grew tired of watching the sunset, especially over the water.

It didn't matter whether he was at the ocean, or this big lake. Sunset was the only time he seemed to be able to clear his mind from the clutter, leaving nothing but awe. This night, the awe was replaced by anticipation of the task ahead.

Now that it was dark and the bugs buzzed his ears relentlessly, his attention was diverted to the tree line, finding what he sought – the glow of the gunmen's fire pit. Hunter checked his revolvers for the freedom of their mechanics by spinning the loaded cylinders then stopping them quickly, being aware of the sound that might carry. He broke the shotgun, the little brass balls stared back at him from the center of the shells, confirming their readiness for the welcome strike of the firing pin. He slid it back into his side-holder and mounted his horse turning north, then east toward the tree line. He entered the woods, still upwind from the camp, dismounted, and carelessly tied Zeke to a skinny branch of a scrub oak.

"If I don't make it back, boy, you pull loose and move on."

The horse nickered like he understood as the half-breed soundlessly made his way through the thicket toward the gunmen's camp. Hunter purposely positioned himself to the north of the encampment. There was a steady warm breeze tonight, and the gunslinger could already smell the sweaty leather from the horses and their riders, the odor getting stronger as he moved closer through the brush. He approached, swift but silent with one pistol drawn, stopped, and went to one knee behind a pine tree surrounded by some palmetto bushes when he heard voices. From this position, Hunter could see them clearly, as they ate metal plates of beans, talking and sharing whiskey.

"One more day's ride and we should be at the home front," said one Cracker as he bent down to the fire, pulling from it a burning stick, and lighting his cigar.

"Well, it's about damn time," complained a red leg. "We been pushin' hard, and I'd like to know why?"

"When Montgomery tells you to do somethin', you don't ask why," replied the Cracker.

There it was, thought Hunter. A bead of sweat rolled down his cheek when he heard Montgomery's name, and he continued to ear-drop.

"You must have an idear why we been called back in such a rush?"

"Rumor is that the half-breed, namely Hunter James Dolin, is alive and comin' for Montgomery."

"I killed lots of men," boasted the red leg. "One more Injun won't matter none. Maybe Montgomery ain't so tough as they say?"

"This ain't no normal Injun; he's partway white after his father; means he's smarter than a normal Injun. He killed fifty men and burned the city of Myakka to the ground. Montgomery wants him dead once and for all. Now let's git' some sleep – Jimmy, you take first watch. I'll spell ya after a while."

"Ah, shit," complained the young man as he threw his empty bean plate at the fire before grabbing his rifle and moving toward the corner of the camp.

"And stay awake," yelled the man after him. "I don't want no surprises."

The Red Legs were chuckling at the young man as they settled down into their bedrolls. They didn't like taking orders from these southern boys, but they were far from home and needed them to get where they were going, so they would eat crow for now.

Hunter James was a patient man, making it fairly easy for him to stay where he was and wait for these men to sleep. He passed the time in thought; *Montgomery knew he was coming. This was unfortunate, but changed nothing.*

The gunslinger was going to kill Richard Montgomery, and anyone else who got in his way, starting with these five men.

CHAPTER TEN

She walked down the gang plank with her head held high, wearing a beautiful low cut, white summer dress, the little frilly matching umbrella spinning above her long auburn hair. A green pearl necklace that matched her eyes perfectly lay upon her heaving bosom. The captain was standing behind her in the doorway and, for a brief moment, he actually thought he saw a gentle smile on Montgomery's face – something he had never seen before.

Her birth name was Helen Beckum, she was born in Kansas nineteen years ago, to a poor pig farmer. Her mother had died from fever when she was twelve, and her father died two days after her sixteenth birthday. Helen lived and kept up the farm as long as she could, until the food ran out. Helen took the few belongings she had and walked for days to the only other place she knew, the town of Topeka. Being a beautiful young girl, she soon found a job at the local whorehouse.

That was where Richard Montgomery found her. He could not believe the resemblance; this girl could be Lilith's twin. With his power and wealth, Richard gave the proprietor of the brothel an offer he could not refuse; one Helen was unable to refuse, as well.

They were soon married and changed her name to Lilith Montgomery. She did not understand why her first name must also be changed, and dared not ask. Richard treated her well enough for the times, though she felt like a prisoner. At least now, she only had to sleep with one man, and he was rich and clean. So she played along, filling her china doll role until something better might come along.

Richard took her hand as she reached out and stepped onto the dock from the ship's plank.

"Thank you, my husband," Helen said, like an actress playing her part.

"You look beautiful, my dear, I take it your voyage was uneventful?" Montgomery glared at the captain as he said this.

"I assure you," said the captain, "other than some rough seas, she's in the same shape as when you saw her last, like I said."

"I'm fine," replied Lilith. "Just a little cabin fever, and having been surrounded by those drunken sailors. I could use a hot bath, though."

"Certainly, my dear, come with me. Captain, you and your men stay on the boat tonight. We'll make other arrangements in the morn."

"Bring your purse with yah, we need to settle up payment before one box is unloaded off this here steamer," spouted the captain.

"In the mornin', Captain, in the mornin'." With a wave of his hand, Richard and Lilith walked up the dock toward the main house as the sun was setting to the west.

"Yes sir, Mr. Montgomery," yelled the captain after them as they moved along. He then spoke quietly to himself, "For now, Monty, I'll play along, for now."

◆ ❖ ◆

An hour had passed, bringing on full dark. A cloudy night, which kept any light from the moon and stars from breaking through, gave Hunter an advantage for his sneak attack. He had not moved from his position, staying totally silent. He could barely hear the drunken snores coming from the sleeping men lying around the campfire through the loud chatter of the crickets.

The half-breed firmly gripped the thirteen-inch Bowie knife as he removed it from his belt and quietly began moving through the brush. He must take out the young man unlucky enough to pull first watch without waking the others, or his little ambush could turn bad. All hell was eventually going to break loose either way.

Hunter moved in the direction where the cowhand had gone over an hour ago, stopping in his tracks only once to the sounds of the whippoorwill. He came around a large pine tree where he spotted the lookout sitting on a fallen tree log, head down, dozing on and off. With his back to Hunter and his head bobbing up and down to fight off sleep, the gunslinger snuck up behind him, timing it perfectly. As the man's head came up in his battle against nodding off, Hunter covered his mouth with his left hand and cut his throat with the big knife, all in one swift motion.

The man moaned and struggled for a few seconds as the warm blood spewed from his jugular vein. His body went completely slack; Hunter laid him down gently and respectfully, face-first into the mud that was mixed with his own warm fluid.

The gunslinger wiped the red smear from his knife on the back of the dead man's shirt before moving toward the others who lay by the fire. With the blade in his right fist, he pulled his left-handed Colt, and using his thumb, he pulled back the hammer. With the speed and skill of a warrior, the gunslinger went to the closest sleeping man.

One horizontal thrust buried the knife in his ear – the man lived long enough to let out a short cry which woke two of the others. As they scrambled to their feet, the half-breed gunned them down without hesitation. The four *bangs* of the Colt 44 spooked some of the horses from their tethers. Hunter had to sidestep one as they scampered past him and through the woods.

The flash from the igniting powder affected his night vision for just a moment. As his sight came back to him, he noticed an empty bedroll to his right.

At that instant, he heard a stick *snap* behind him. The gunslinger turned and fired his last two bullets into the chest of a shadow appearing through the brush. As the man was falling, he fired his revolver hitting Hunter in the side, dropping him to one knee. Hunter yelled out as pain shot through his belly, only the tail-end of his outcry being heard over the sound of the gunfire. He pushed to his feet; holding his side, he walked over to the dead man who was lying on his back.

"You son-of-a-bitch!" he scolded, along with a swift kick to the man's body. "Dammit," he exclaimed, wincing from the movement.

Hunter took notice that the old cowhand's pants were hanging half way down his thigh, his finger still holding onto the belt loop. *Just bad luck,* he thought. Obviously, this fellow went to relieve himself while Hunter was relieving the guard of his life.

The gunslinger walked carefully over to the fire, reloading the Colt with a new cartridge as he went. Using the light from the flames, he removed his shirt to inspect the gunshot wound. Lucky for him, the bullet went all the way through, but he was bleeding badly. He shoved his Bowie knife into the hot coals of the fire with the one hand; with the other, he held pressure on the bullet hole, the blood still poured over his fingers and ran down his back.

The wound was about two and a half inches in and off the hipbone, and just above the beltline; the slug had missed any vital organs. The gunslinger knew he would survive, since this new injury was about an inch away from a scar he had received some years back from a disgruntled gambler. The memory reminded him of the pain he was about to endure.

He began rummaging around the camp until he found what he was looking for. Popping the cork, he chugged the whiskey several times until he depleted half the bottle. Hunter took several deep breaths then dowsed the front and the back of the wound with the alcohol. The sting forced a growl to escape between his clenched teeth, dropping him to his knees at the fire. He fought the dizziness by taking another long swig from the bottle. Then he removed the red glowing knife from the coals and slapped the flat part to the exit hole in his back – the growls became screams, as he fought to stay conscious.

He quickly turned the blade and slapped it to the front, where the bullet had entered. The sizzle of his skin could be heard. He lacked the energy to manage another scream on his way to unconsciousness; but before blacking out, his last memory would be the smell of his own burning flesh.

CHAPTER ELEVEN

The blue moonlight shone through the cross-shaped slits carved in the wooden shutters onto her lovely face as she slept. Hunter never felt more blessed than he did at this moment, as he admired her beauty. They had made love many times that night, each time more intense than the last. It seemed that everything was going to be all right, until the rifles poked through the cross-slits in every window. The order to fire rang out, just before the bullets shredded her to a bloody death.

Hunter woke up suddenly, jumping violently to his feet, instantaneously pulling both revolvers from their holsters ready to kill. He had no idea where he was or how the blazes he got there.

"Easy simmer, easy simmer, son," said a voice.

Hunter could now see someone sitting by a small fire through the sweat running down his brow, "Matt? Is that you?"

"It's Jebediah, good to see you up and about."

Hunter looked around for the bodies of the men he had killed as his memory came flashing back to him, along with the pain from his wound. He then realized he was in a camp, but not in the same part of the woods where the battle had taken place. He turned, suddenly cocking his pistols, as a branch snapped behind him.

Walt came out of the darkness into the fire light, messing with his belt being smothered underneath his belly. "Don't shoot me, Hunter James. I'm stopped up, and if you shoot me in the gut, I warn yah, it'll be messy," said the old coot with a chuckle as he sat down in front of the fire with a groan.

Hunter put his guns away then wiped the sweat from his face. "What the hell are you guys doin' here?" Hunter winced and grabbed his side.

"Pure luck," said Jebediah. "We just happened to come across yah."

The gunslinger took a few steps and sat down easily by Jebediah. Walt leaned across the fire and handed him a jug. Hunter took a long draw, the shine made his head tighten and shake from side to side. "What in God's name is this?"

"That's Okeechobee whiskey right there; good ain't it?" Walt said proudly with a smile. "That's my special brew. Drink up; I got plenty more where that comes from."

Hunter took another draw. "Damn, that's better than moonshine."

"Better than sunshine," replied Jeb.

"Sure better than a rainy day," added Walt.

The three men broke out in laughter; Hunter instantly grabbed his side as pain shot through it, making them laugh even harder. All three men were feeling right good being together again. Jebediah and Walt had been friends for many years and now they felt that same camaraderie with the young half-breed.

To Hunter, the two old coots reminded him of his friend Matt; but the violins didn't last long; it was back to the real world and the job at hand.

"All right, enough," said Hunter. "Tell me about it."

Jebediah and Walt looked at each other in hesitation.

Hunter told them, "I don't give a damn who tells the story; I just need to know if I got to go back there and clean up that mess."

Jebediah spoke up, like a kid seeking approval, "Well, the horses were long gone when we come across ya; we sunk the bodies in a sinking hole along with the saddles on top for weight. We took what food they had and a few other things, but nothin' with no markins' on it."

Hunter smiled a little; he was really enjoying the company of these two like usual. After a slight pause, he said, "I don't have the...words."

"No need," said Walt, "I just hope we did ya a goodin'. By the time anyone finds them, this whole thing will be over."

"What's for supper?" Hunter asked.

"Well we already et," answered Walt, "but I got some bear meat, and a story to go along with it that you ain't gonna' believe."

The weathered old timers told Hunter all about the grizzly they tracked and killed in the swamps. They went on and on, laughing, drinking shine, and eating bear steaks. It was the most fun these boys could remember having in a long time. The Okeechobee whiskey was a natural pain-killer and was doing its job on Hunter's wound; his temperature felt normal and his gut feeling told him there was no infection. The gunslinger had so many scars at this time in his life he could not count them all if he were standing naked in a room with mirrored walls.

The worst of these healed wounds was his left middle finger, a quarter of an inch shorter than the other; it had been shot off two years back in a gunfight on a trail in north Florida. It had been a fair trade, the tip of his finger for the lives of five bad men. The Colt revolver no longer noticed his left hand's disability, for it now shot as straight and true as it did before its misfortune. The only time Hunter noticed his missing nub was when it itched, bringing back limited memories.

When a man had killed as many men as Hunter James Dolin, he could surely not keep them straight. Knowing that every man he killed was justified, he no longer gave his actions a second thought. Life was tough, most men were evil, and he would act accordingly.

Hunter was the first to sleep and the whiskey would not allow him to dream, which was a good thing for his dreams usually turned to nightmares.

The old coots drifted off shortly afterward and only luck kept them from being slaughtered in their sleep. As diligent as these men were, the alcohol diluted their senses this night, catching them with their guard down to give them the best rest they'd had in weeks.

◆❖◆

Jebidiah and Walt woke at the crack of dawn to the smell of frying lard.

Hunter had arisen earlier and raided a few Mallard nests built among the cattails on the edge of a small lake, located less than a mile from their camp. He did not take all the eggs from the momma ducks; he took only a few from each as was normal practice for hunters and gatherers of the land. Most men who live off the land instinctively know their survival depends on conservation.

The three men drank coffee with their eggs, conversing not at all until their heads cleared from the night's drink.

Jebediah was the first to speak. "So tell me son, back in Myakka did you find Scooter?"

The gunslinger pulled three hand-rolled cigarillos from his pouch and tossed them one after the other over to his friends.

In return they nodded a thank ya'.

"I found him. Justice was done."

"That's good," said Walt, "That mealy mouth weasel deserved whatever he got comin' to him."

"So where does that leave yah, son?" asked Jebediah. "Have you come to peace?"

"No, not at all," replied Hunter. "In fact, it's worse than that, before I dropped Scooter head first into a gator pit, he told me a little tale."

"Jesus," whispered Walt. "*Lus-tee Manito Nak-nee.*"

"Say what?" asked Hunter with a glare.

Walt showed signs of embarrassment for a moment. "*Lus-tee Manito Nak-nee...* You know, black spirit man... Oh, never mind."

"Anyways," Hunter continued, "Richard Montgomery lives; and those dead bodies you two sunk back there in the swamp proves that."

"Holy shit!" said Walt.

"Damn!" said Jebediah, in unison.

"Knowin' Montgomery, I'm sure he's got a small army in that lake house, and he knows I'm alive."

"Son, I can't even begin to know what you're feelin', but I know what you're thinkin'. Why don't you just ride on out a here? North Carolina's got swamp fit to live in, if you don't mind a little cold."

"Ever been to Louisiana, Hunter James? They gots beautiful swamp there, son. We'll go with yah," chimed in Walt.

Hunter stared at the old men seated across from him for a time. Then he stood and began packing his gear, before he replied, "You know I can't and won't do that. There are debts to be paid, and destiny has made me the collector."

Jebediah stood and began packing his things; Walt did the same. They all did this in silence until their camp was cleaned up, and they were in the saddle.

"This is my fight. You all don't need to be doin' this."

The old timers just stared at the gunslinger without uttering a word.

"Damned old fools," said Hunter as he led them from the woods toward the trail. Only God knew how they would end up, and the Lord surely cared more than they did.

CHAPTER TWELVE

Montgomery's home front was at a full buzz, now that *The Miss Lilly* and her cargo had arrived. The ship was built primarily to transport Richard's belongings from the north; he had sold all his land in the Dakotas, acres and acres of mining camps. The claims were played out, but he purposely put some gold back into the ground and spread it along the streams and banks, giving the impression of richness. He had pulled a wagon of gold out of the claims and then sold the barren land for a good price.

Richard Montgomery was nothing but an evil killer, disguised as a businessman. He had acquired the lands by force, making the miners and tin pans sell at a cheap price, or else. The ones that would not relent had met with horrible accidents or simply disappeared, but somehow always seemed to sign over their claims to Montgomery just prior.

That morning, Montgomery settled up with the captain as promised. The captain took his payment and stowed the iron box of coins away in his quarters, that man was assuredly all about gold.

"Stick with me, Captain," boasted Richard from his seat in the ship's galley. "If you live through this war, you could retire a very rich man."

"Oh, I plan on livin' and I plan on bein' rich. But which war you talkin' bout, the one between the States or with Hunter James Dolin?"

The two men stared at each other for a time. The captain walked over to a cabinet, pulled out a bottle of whiskey and two glasses. He sat down across from Richard and poured them both half-full.

"I don't know how you came by that information, but I had hoped to keep a lid on it until I was ready."

"Word travels fast in these parts. I heard about a man named Scooter Johnson, then I saw you pullin' all your men back here. I said to myself the War Between the States ain't comin' this far south, hell, they got no interest in any swamp, anyhow. So I put two and two together, and it had that half-breed written all over it."

Both men tipped their glasses back, one after the other. The sun had been up for an hour now, making sipping time over. The captain poured the glasses nearly full this time.

"What do you know of the half-breed?"

"I know what I heard," replied the captain. "I know the Army had a price on his head before the war drew the soldiers out of Florida. They wanted him for killin' fifty men and burnin' down Myakka City. I also know he'd been missin' for a year 'til someone gunned down Scooter Johnson's hired guns at his saloon. Scooter was one of your men – seen him lately?"

Richard tipped back his glass and smacked his lips. "Two of my boys found some pieces of him in a gator pit just outside the city."

"Shit," was all the captain could say before lighting his pipe.

"Don't fret. I won't underestimate him this time. I've got better men, and I got *The Miss Lilly* and her Gatlin guns."

"You always were arrogant, Richard," replied the captain, blowing out smoke that began to fill the small room. "Someday it's gonna' catch up with yah. I always said that. I just hope it's not this time, while I'm around."

Richard Montgomery stood, adjusting his gunbelt. "You just worry 'bout my boat, and I'll worry 'bout the half-breed. I think under the circumstances you and your crew should stay on the ship."

"I agree."

"If you need anything, you send one of your boys to the house and I'll take care of it."

"Oh, I will take you up on that, don't you worry."

Richard nodded and left the steamer. He didn't trust this man completely, but he would have to rely on him for now. The half-breed gunslinger was coming for him and he needed as many guns as his money would buy.

Lilith had washed up from her morning wifely duties, and she was now dressed and watching out the front window of the master bedroom. Looking out upon the lake through the oak trees, she could see the dock and the ramp of the steamship. Richard walked down the gangplank, and stood on the dock, lighting a cigar. Lilith did not like her husband; she knew he was just plain bad, one of those men born rotten to the core.

She would continue to play along, waiting for her opportunity to escape. She knew he would hunt her down and kill her before letting her go. Richard Montgomery would have to die for her to be free. On more than one occasion, she had hovered over him with a knife as he lay passed out from too much whiskey. But she could not go through with it, she was simply too afraid of him and his power.

Lilith watched Montgomery talking to two of his men on the head of the dock. She knew something was going on, she had heard rumors of a half-Indian who had killed many men, and this was why everyone was on alert. She did not know why this half-breed wanted Richard dead – she did not care – she only hoped he was good enough to get through this small army. But she couldn't see how it was possible for one man. Lilith decided, in that very moment, that she would help this

Indian any way she could, if the opportunity ever presented itself.

A Lilith jumped, startled, as a knock came at the door. "Mrs. Montgomery?"

"Yes, who's there?"

"Mr. Montgomery would like you downstairs for vittles."

"Be right down." She gathered herself quickly and left the room for the staircase and the first floor kitchen.

Richard and Lilith dined together in the eating area off the kitchen. There were many wood tables and chairs in the dining area. They were seated at a larger table in the corner, reserved for Richard Montgomery. He always ate amongst his men – back against the wall – watching as they walked in and out from the kitchen, full plates coming out, empty plates going in.

The men glanced carefully at Lilith, trying to get a look without Montgomery noticing them. They could not help themselves, for Lilith was the most beautiful woman most of them had ever seen. Florida was no-man's-land and she was a highfalutin' northern city girl. Not to mention, the closest whorehouse was three days ride and the boys had been stuck here for two weeks now, protecting the home front.

There were all sorts of men here, who thought very different about women. Some thought of saving Lilith's life and receiving from her a hero's reward. There were other men here, the worst ones, who daydreamed of finding her alone and raping her violently. Then, there were others who minded their own business – only looking to do their job and draw their pay. These were usually the seasoned old timers and the most danger-ous.

Montgomery fed his men well, regardless of type. He had acquired a professional cook who lived in a small room just off the dining area and the kitchen was open twenty-four hours.

Chinn Yang had been down this road before – he had worked for a man named Frank Lugar who owned a ranch outside Myakka City. Chinn was one of the few who survived the wrath of the half-breed gunslinger, only because the half-breed did not run across him. Chinn knew how to make himself scarce. He was fluent in the English language, but he never spoke it, that's why he was still alive. Chinn Yang had been a slave ever since he was a young boy, brought to this country from China to lay track for the railroad. These were the same trains being successfully used by the Union against the Confederacy in a war which was far from civil.

Chinn Yang was making his way from the kitchen to the dining room with a tray of bread and butter for Montgomery. He had made it to the corner table when the Chinese cook was pushed aside by a very large bearded man with a single, worn handled revolver hanging from his hip. He was middle-aged, weathered, and rugged.

He stood across the table from Montgomery, towering over the seated Richard, giving him the advantage. "I'll have a word with you, Montgomery."

Richard looked up from his plate and continued to cut a generous piece of steak; he jabbed it with a large knife and put it in his mouth after dipping it into the runny yolk of his egg. He continued to eat very calmly, as the egg dripped from his mustache. "You reek of liquor, sir. Are you sure you want to interrupt my mornin' meal?" asked Richard Montgomery.

"My name is Willy Macoy, and I'm callin' you out."

Montgomery stopped eating; he set his utensils down and glared at this man before him as he wiped his mouth with a piece of linen while leaning comfortably against the back of his chair. A long pause followed as their eyes locked, several men slowly moved in behind Montgomery resting their hands on the butts of their guns.

"You work for me, Mister?" asked Montgomery.

"About a week now, just to git close to yah. Now are we goin' outside, or right here's fine by me?" The man's voice broke a little as he spoke, he had thought about this moment day and night for two years, and now it had finally arrived.

"What's your problem with me?" asked Richard in his best innocent voice. "I'm only a business man these days."

"You killed my family and stole their gold claim back in the Dakotas, just past two years ago today. I'm here for a gentleman's Justice."

"I assure you, you've got the wrong man, but I can see there is no talkin' you out of it." Richard pointed his hand toward the door. "After you, we shall take this outside."

The man turned on his heel and took three steps toward the door.

Montgomery stood up, pulled his revolver, and shot the man in the back of the head. As the bullet exited his left eye socket, the man seemed to stand at attention for a moment before timbering like a falling tree, hitting the ground with a *thud* on the floorboards, his face breaking his fall. A puddle of warm blood quickly formed around his head.

Montgomery holstered his gun, the smoke from his firearm rising slowly up to the ceiling. "Anybody else got a problem with me?" Montgomery shouted.

There was no reply from anyone as Richard scanned the room; most went back to their breakfast. Chinn Yang served the bread and left the room for the safety of his kitchen as several of Richard's men went over to remove the body.

"Leave him," barked Richard, as he sat down and continued eating the rare steak in front of him. He glanced often at the dead man, as the blood soaked into the cracks of the wood floor.

Lilith was glued to her seat during this whole episode, she now stood and scrambled from the room in disgust.

"Where the hell you goin'?" shouted Richard as he chewed on the red meat.

"Want me to git her back here, Mr. Montgomery?" asked Bodie from the doorway, as Lilith scooted past him as he entered.

"No, let her go. You know how women are; their soft emotions can't handle what men must do."

Bodie walked over to the dead man on the floor, He kneeled down and grabbed a handful of hair, turning the head toward him.

"Did you hire this man, Bodie?" asked Richard.

"Well, he ain't got much of a face left, but I recognize him and you know I do most of the hiring 'round here."

Bodie stood and pointed to two of the men. "Git this body out a here. Throw it under the house – them gators might as well start gittin' use to human meat." As he said this, he looked in Montgomery's direction. "I have a feelin' they'll be gittin' more bodies in the near future."

Richard said nothing, he just went on back to his food, but the half-breed gunslinger did enter his mind for the first time that day.

♦❖♦

Lilith walked halfway down the dock trying to get as far away from the dining room as possible. Two men with rifles followed her, but kept their distance as they had been previously ordered.

She stopped and stared out onto the lake, leaning on the handrail in thought. Richard was mistaken, the blood and killing did not bother her at all, she'd seen it her whole life, and the only thing that bothered her was that Montgomery was still alive. That man was brave coming here but he never stood a chance. Richard Montgomery was an evil sort and didn't fight fair.

Her only hope was the half-breed, but where was he? And who was he? The odds were obviously against him, Richard's men were waiting at the ready. If the Indian man came and all hell broke loose, she decided that's when she would make her escape. Lilith had no idea where she would go, but any place was better than here. Even though she was pampered and well-fed, she still did not have her freedom.

CHAPTER THIRTEEN

Hunter, Jebediah, and Walt traveled south, a mile inland from the big lake's shore, keeping to the thicket. They moved along cautiously through the swamp and stopped frequently while Hunter used the spyglass searching for signs of Montgomery's home. The terrain changed from woods to swamp and back again; only once did they have to maneuver into hiding by ducking down into the palm meadows as a five-man band of Red Legs rode up their flank.

The Red Legs were moving fast and passed by them without discovery. Hunter and his small, but mature, army followed in their tracks at a slower pace, which took them closer to the shoreline. Hunter suddenly came to an abrupt stop. Purposely, there were two horse lengths between Jebediah and Hunter, and two between Jebediah and Walt. These men and their animals had traveled long distances and they worked together well.

They all waited in silence as Hunter pulled his scope from his saddlebag and, putting it to his eye, he scanned the countryside from center to the left, then slowly back to center, then to the right where he stayed, moving little. It was obvious to all there was something interesting in his sights.

Hunter put away the spyglass and began checking his guns. Jebediah looked back to Walt making eye contact. Without a word, the two men brought their horses alongside Hunter, placing him in the center.

"When you check them guns, trouble usually seems to follow," said Jebediah.

"Shit," groaned Walt.

The gunslinger said nothing; He sheathed his Colts then pulled the sawed-off from his side-holster and broke it, checking the shells for moisture. Satisfied he was locked and loaded, he put the shotgun away and took out the spyglass, handing it to Jebediah. "Take a look."

Jeb put the scope to his left eye, but not liking that one, he moved it to the right one.

"You know which eye to close on that thing?" Walt joked with a snicker.

"Quiet, you old coot," replied Jebediah, pointing it in the direction of the smoke that could be seen over the trees. "Looks more like a fortress than a house."

"Follow the walkout to the lake – at the end of the dock," said Hunter.

"Son-of-a-bitch," cursed Jebediah. "Them are Gatlin' guns on that steamer. I don't know – we might be bitin' off more than we can chew."

"Let me see that thing," demanded Walt.

Jebediah handed the glass to Hunter, who then handed it to Walt, who then looked in the same direction. "I shore don't like it much boys," warned Walt. "There's a small Army down yonder, and them Gatlin's can do a lot of damage. I seen 'em in the Indian wars, cutting' down whole war parties like nothin'."

"Changin' your minds, boys?" asked Hunter.

"Well, I didn't ride all this way for nothin'. What do you say, Walt?" asked Jebediah.

Walt was still looking through the scope when his jaw fell open dramatically before he answered, "I don't think we're goin' in there anytime soon, not without a plan any ways,"

Hunter took the glass from Walt and began scanning.

"Second floor balcony, center of the house," directed Walt.

The gunslinger found what Walt was talking about and he could not believe his eyes. There, on the second floor landing, stood Lilith – *no, not his Lilith* – but the woman could have been her twin. Hunter could not believe it; Montgomery went out and found a girl the spittin' image of her. Feelings flooded back on Hunter. He handed the spyglass to Jebediah, who was wondering what the devil they were talking about. He did a double take through the glass,

"I only saw her once," said Jeb. "A long time back, but it sure looks like her." Jebediah closed the scope, turning his attention to the gunslinger. "Could it be?"

"No," replied Hunter. "I saw her die. I'll bet this woman is not there of her own free will, just like Lilith. I got to save her."

"I think I need a drink," said Walt.

"It will be dark soon," said Hunter, ignoring Walt's comment. "We'll fall back in the swamp and set up a safe camp. Most of Montgomery's men are Yankee Red Legs and they won't look for us back in there. Let's move."

They headed deep in the swamp 'til they found a hammock cluttered with trees, a good mile and a half away from Montgomery's house. Hunter and the old men went to work clearing out a spot in the center of the small island. Hunter built a wall from the cut branches, weaving them together with the efficiency of a Lower Creek Indian woman. This wall would shield the light of their fire from being seen in the night for the cooking.

Jebediah and Walt devoured bear steaks, washing it down with the Okeechobee whiskey. Hunter ate little meat and passed on the moonshine, for his night was just beginning. He'd been thinking hard on his next move since he saw that woman on the balcony.

"I'm goin' in alone, boys," explained the half-breed as he pulled his bow and arrows from the Appaloosa's saddle.

"You want us to sit here and do nothin'?" asked Walt, clear bewilderment in his voice.

"I want you two to git some rest, stay somewhat sober, and be ready in case I got men riding my ass when we git back here."

"We?" asked Jebediah, knowing damn well and good what the gunslinger was up to.

Hunter ignored the question as he stripped Zeke of his saddle, down to the horse's bare back. He removed his shirt and his boots; he then laced up a pair of knee-high moccasins he removed from one of his saddlebags. Hanging the bow over one shoulder and the quiver of arrows over the other, he jumped up on his horse. Hunter carried only one revolver, which he tucked in his front belt next to the thirteen-inch Bowie knife.

"God speed, son," said Jebediah.

"Watch your ass," said Walt.

The half-breed gunslinger rode off into the darkness, heading for Montgomery's lakefront fortress. For a split second the thought crossed Hunter's mind: *Would he see these two old coots ever again?*

For Walt and Jebediah this same thought did not just cross their minds, but would linger there until his return. The old men found themselves checking their guns, a habit of the gunslinger's that would give them something to do while they waited. Walt and Jebediah thought to pack up the camp and prepare their horses for a quick retreat. They would then sleep for a short time, rebuilding their energy; old men needed their rest, or something Walt liked to call his 'purty sleep'.

Hunter and Zeke moved swiftly and quietly through the swamp and forest. As he went over the plan in his head, he concluded it was simple, but sound. His success would depend on how his adversaries would react. He did not think they would suspect he would come in and kidnap the woman; not even Montgomery could predict that.

Some might think Hunter was a romantic, but this could not be farther from the truth – revenge was what he sought. Hurting Montgomery was his main objective; but the fact this woman could be Lilith's twin most likely drove him to this decision. The gunslinger pushed these thoughts from his mind as he came upon the edge of the woods at the clearing.

He dismounted and tied Zeke's reins loosely to a scrub oak. The half-breed was barely a shadow moving along the tree line toward the lake. As he went, he glanced at the rear balcony where he had seen the woman earlier in the day, but he saw nothing. Now the middle of the night, there were no lights on in that part of the house – if she was not asleep in her room, the plan would fail.

Hunter was still looking about when he spotted two guards on the roof of the house and a third guard on the second floor balcony, walking the perimeter. The man slowly walked around the building with a rifle in his mitts and a cigar dangling from his mouth. Hunter squatted in the brush, counting the seconds it took the man to circle the building. Just over a minute and a half from the woman's door, around the house, and back to the door again.

The gunman stopped; he opened one side of the double doors and peered in for a short time. Seeming satisfied, he closed it and began his walk around the balcony in the opposite direction from where he came.

Hunter left his position and headed to the front of the house toward the lake. There were two guards spread out on the hundred-foot walkout to the dock, and two more that he could see on the steam ship.

He could hear the sounds of a poker game going on from the candle lit first floor in the front of the stilt house. This was a sound Hunter knew well but had not heard in a long time as the poker chips *clicked* in the night. He suddenly yearned for the days when poker was his living. He reminisced about the good old days of smoke-filled saloons, and the whiskey that flowed down his gullet as if funneled. His thoughts were broken when the front door opened and a man walked out onto the balcony, a glass in one hand and a stogie in the other.

To Hunter's surprise, he recognized Richard Montgomery. He stood like a statue, no more than thirty yards from the gunslinger, looking out over the lake. Hunter took his bow from around his neck and shoulder; he loaded an arrow and then pulled back the string, locking his forearm to a deadly aim. Hunter had his sights on the neck of Montgomery, just to the right of his large Adams apple. At this distance the arrow would enter his throat in the front and right out the back; only the fletching made of feathers would keep it from going all the way through. Seconds went by, and then more seconds, both men were perfectly still, Hunter had the arrow drawn back and locked; all he had to do was loose the arrow, and Montgomery was a dead man.

Richard Montgomery shot back his drink and took a draw off his cigar, then he threw the butt over the rail as he turned on his heel, and walked back into the house.

The gunslinger lowered his bow as a drop of sweat ran down his cheek. If Walt and Jebediah were there beside him, they would have asked: *Why didn't you shoot the bastard?* Hunter would have said: *Not that way, I want it to be up close and personal, I want to look into his eyes when I take his life and I want him to see me.*

Hunter knew the time was now; he turned on his knee from his crouched position toward the lake and pulled a piece of cloth from his belt loop, wrapping it around the arrowhead. He lit it with a match that he struck off his pant-leg in an upward motion. Hunter loaded and loosed the arrow. It flew through the trees, hitting the steamship at the top of its wheelhouse. The dry, painted wood caught fire immediately, catching the attention of the two boat guards first and then the men on the dock, who took off running toward the ship.

The house came alive with quite a commotion as a bell began to ring. Men poured out of the house, some with buckets, headed toward the lake and the burning ship.

By this time, the half-breed was already at the back of the house, climbing the giant oak. Hunter walked the length of a large branch and jumped down onto the first floor porch. He pulled his Colt from his belt, cocked it, then kicked in the back door, and entered the room. He came face to face with the woman. She was striking to him, as she stood there in her white undergarments – so much like his Lilith, it was mindboggling. There were slight differences he could now see; the woman had jumped when he made his crashing entrance, with only a slight gasp escaping her throat.

She did not flee but just stood there, staring back at him.

After a moment, Hunter asked, "Are you going to come quietly or am I going to have to throw you over this balcony?"

"You're him..." said the woman. "You're the half-breed."

"We need to go, now!" replied the gunslinger.

She grabbed her dress off the back of a chair, walked past him, and out the door. Hunter walked to the large bed and yanked the top sheet by the corner dragging it out the back. He quickly and efficiently tied it to the rail and threw it over the side next to where the woman waited patiently. Hunter put his revolver in his belt after looking around for guards. Then, without saying a word, he helped her over the rail.

She looked into his eyes, pausing as they were face to face, before she climbed down the sheet.

He watched her descend, noting her ability. Hunter looked around again, but there was no one to be seen. They were all out by the lake, fighting the fire as he had planned; but they must hurry. As soon as they discovered the arrow, they would come for him. He flung himself over the side, bending his knees as he should to avoid breakage. He landed on his feet, making the twelve-foot drop with ease. The gunslinger and the woman hit the ground at the same time.

"We got to go," insisted Hunter.

She accepted his hand and they ran as fast as she could for the dark seclusion of the woods, fading into the swamp beyond.

♦ ❖ ♦

The fire was extinguished fairly quickly, due to the men's quick action with their buckets of lake water.

Montgomery made it down the dock and to the ship, arriving as the last splash from a bucket hit the side of the steamer.

"Which one of you drunkin' fools was sleepin' on the job allowin' my ship to catch fire?"

"My men don't sleep on the job," said the captain as he walked up to Richard.

"Well, what the hell happened?" demanded Montgomery.

"I think it has begun..." replied the captain. He handed Richard the tail end of an arrow with the feathers singed.

Montgomery stared at the burnt stick in his hand, rolling it as if to see what was on the other side. "*Son-of-a-bitch!* It's the half-breed."

There were men scattered about on the boat, on the dock, and up the walkway.

"Bodie!" shouted Richard.

"Here, boss." Bodie was coming up the walk, strapping on his guns as he maneuvered through the men.

"Where the hell have you been?"

"It was my down time, sir. I just came off a fifteen-hour shift."

Montgomery slammed the broken arrow into Bodies hand. "Git these men in gear and find him."

"All right, boys!" shouted Bodie. "Spread out and check the grounds, check the house, and watch your ass. You all know by now who we're dealing with."

The men dispersed into action, pulling their weapons as they began their search. Birdie was joining in with the rest of the men, eager to get into the fight.

Bodie stopped him after five steps down the boardwalk. "Birdie boy, you stay here with me."

With a sigh of disappointment, the boy stopped and holstered his gun.

Bodie turned back to Montgomery. "What do you think, boss?"

"I think that savage tried to burn up my battleship."

"One lit arrow with guards ten feet away and surrounded by water, looks more like a diversion to me."

"You might just be right on that assumption, Bodie," chimed in the captain.

"A diversion for what purpose?" asked Richard.

"Hey, over here," came a faint yell from the back of the house.

Birdie, Bodie, and Montgomery hurried down the walkway with their guns drawn, leaving the captain behind.

"You two," yelled the captain at the deck guards. "Git on them Gatlin' guns and be ready for my orders."

With Birdie leading the way, the three men came around the building to see the bed sheet hanging from the balcony.

"What the hell?" questioned Richard.

One of his men came out the bedroom door onto the balcony. "She's gone, boss."

Bodie had never seen Montgomery look like this before. His face turned three different shades of red, while sweat broke out from his hairline to run down his face.

Through clenched teeth, Montgomery gave his orders to Bodie, "I want this compound secured, and I want you to put together a hunting party of ten men. I want that son-of-a-bitch half-breed bastard found and killed. A thousand dollars to the man who kills him and brings me his body, or his head!"

"What about the woman?" asked Bodie.

"You mean my wife? Obviously, she's been kidnapped. You will rescue her and bring her back to me."

"Yes sir, of course," replied Bodie, trying not to show his skepticism.

He set Montgomery's men into action securing the big house and putting together a hunting party. Bodie was an excellent tracker and would lead the party himself. The half-breed would have a three-hour head start for they needed daylight to track him and sunup was at least two hours away. Bodie did not think the half-breed would go far, knowing the history between the gunslinger and Montgomery. Many men would die over this pissing contest between these two, but he would continue. This was his job and he was paid well for it. Bodie's bottom line was for him and Birdie boy to get out of this, alive and rich in the end. This was a cutthroat business and everyone with half-a-mind had their own agenda. Other than Richard, Bodie was the only one who knew how much gold was in the house. But there was one other in this bunch Bodie needed to keep one eye on, and he would do so until the end of this little war.

CHAPTER FOURTEEN

Hunter and the woman made their way through the brush and swamp to where the Appaloosa waited. He helped the woman onto Zeke's back; they moved with purpose, but did not hurry. The gunslinger knew they would not begin tracking them until daylight, giving them some time. He walked the horse only so far before he fell back, clearing their tracks from behind. He took a thick stick and pushed around the edges of the hoof prints filling them in with mud, following up with another stick branched out with oak leaves at the ends. A back and forth sweeping motion blended their tracks with the rest of the wet forest floor.

Hunter knew a good tracker would be able to read the ground and continue to follow. His purpose in this was merely to slow them down 'til they reached the knee-deep water of the swamp. They reached the edge of the watery bog as the sun was threatening to rise. Hunter walked the horse through the water, sensing the woman's eyes upon him. Forty feet in and a half-mile to the south of their destination, Hunter mounted the horse behind her, and turned to the northwest.

Their pursuers would eventually find where they had entered the water, but from there they would have to guess in which direction they had fled. The men would be forced to turn back, split up, or wander in the swamps searching aimlessly for days.

Neither the woman nor Hunter had spoken since their departure from Montgomery's stilt home. Her silence and cooperation surprised him a little. He figured right, that she was not staying with Montgomery freely, but he hadn't expected her to come with him so willingly.

The rays of the sun were pushing up over the horizon when the overdue conversation was begun by her.

"Where are you taking me?"

"I have some friends waiting for us on a hammock a few miles from here. They will lead you north, away from this place."

"What if I refuse to go? Hunter James Dolin."

She was still wearing her undergarments and he noticed for the first time that their bodies were rubbing close together; her smell was maddening.

"I would say you don't have a choice," replied Hunter sternly. "Seeing how you know my name, maybe you should tell me yours, ma'am."

"My name is Lilith."

Hunter stopped Zeke in his watery tracks and tried to look her over by leaning back from his hindmost position.

She turned to him, clearly noting the shock and confusion on his face. "That's the name Richard gave me – my birth name is Helen, Helen Beckum."

"He made you change your name to," Hunter paused for a moment and then continued, "*Lilith?*"

"If you know Montgomery, which I have a feeling you do, you know I did not have much choice."

Hunter continued to move Zeke along through the shin high water and knee-high swamp grass. There were a dozen hammocks in sight, spread out for miles in many directions. They turned north and headed for the limestone island of palm trees where Jebediah and Walt were waiting.

"Who was Lilith?" asked Helen, out of nowhere.

"She was my woman – I rescued her from Montgomery, but I could not save her."

"What happened to her?

There was a cry from the sky as a bald eagle soared overhead; a mullet could be seen in its talons. The gunslinger waited for the bird to fly away and become quiet before he answered,

"He killed her with extreme prejudice."

"So now you have taken me," Helen said plainly. "Do you aim to kill me?"

"Why would you think that?" asked Hunter.

"For revenge," she said.

"You feel that I am vengeful?"

"You reek of it."

Hunter stopped Zeke once again.

Helen tensed, waiting for a blade to pierce her side; but it didn't come, much to her relief.

"My intentions are to rescue you," he replied. "No – that's wrong, I mean to save you."

Hunter pulled the reins, changing the Appaloosa's direction toward a medium-sized island that was just one of many strewn across the marshy lands. He dug his heels into Zeke's body, pushing him harder. "Yah, yah," he yelled, making it clear to her he was done talking.

◆❖◆

Bodie, Birdie boy, and eight other heavily armed men began their search at daybreak following the tracks the gunslinger left behind. The horses were fresh; Bodie was in front as the lead tracker and he positioned Birdie in the center of the single file convoy, figuring it to be the safest place for the boy. One man ambushing ten men was unheard of, but Bodie would not put it past the half-breed to try.

Over the last few years, the gunslinger had become a legend in these parts. The stories told of a gun-slinging savage that stood seven-feet tall, killed one hundred men, and then burned an entire city to the ground while avoiding capture from the United States Army and every bounty hunter north, south, east, and west of the Mississippi. The legend was exaggerated, but Bodie knew not by much.

If they could only kill this Hunter James Dolin, with the Civil War winding down and clearing the passages, Bodie and Birdie could take their money owed and move away from the danger of such men as Richard Montgomery.

Bodie had lost his wife and young son to disease many years back. He had wandered through life aimlessly, until he found an orphaned boy barely surviving in the deep woods of the panhandle. Birdie was thirteen then, his parents killed by Indians in the Seminole Indian wars. Bodie took him in as his own and taught him to shoot and survive in the times. Now the boy was seventeen; young, but still a man. Bodie educated him over the years the best he could, the boy had trail smarts more than most. Like most young men his age, Birdie thought he would live forever. As far as Bodie was concerned, it was his job as a stepfather to protect the boy from himself and others.

They followed the gunslinger's trail easily at first, but their progress slowed from his covering of the tracks. Bodie was a veteran in such matters and after some effort was able to continue the pursuit. At one point on the trail, Bodie raised his left arm, bent at the elbow and balling his fingers into a fist, which brought the following men to a halt. He dismounted and, holding on to his horse's reins, he walked slowly, studying the ground at his feet.

"Watch your flank, boys!" shouted Bodie, loud enough for all to hear. "You two watch the front while I'm rootin' down here." said Bodie, to the two men behind him.

The man called Big Joe, directly behind Bodie, pulled his rifle from his saddle-sheath, cocked it, and rested it on his shoulder as he looked intently forward, scanning the trail up ahead. This sent a wave of pulls and clicks of revolvers, shotguns, and rifles through the line of men that ran clear to the last one at the rear. There was a reason Bodie placed Big Joe second in line behind him. Bodie knew from wars past that Joe was a serious man and would watch his back.

"They changed direction here," Bodie said aloud to no one in-particular, from his crouched position. "I feel we're gainin' on um," he said to everyone, "so keep some extra wits about yah."

Climbing back in the saddle, Bodie led his men in their new direction for several miles, until the flow of tracks ran dry – or wet in this case – for they ended at the edge of the marsh that stretched as far as the eye could see, and then some.

"Shit!" exclaimed Bodie.

The men fanned out coming alongside their leader, bringing their horses to the edge of the water. Some of them drank from their canteens; others took the time to light up.

"What the hell we gonna' do now, Bode?" asked Big Joe.

"Well, there's no way to track them in this high water, if he was careful which I have no doubt he was. The grass that parted for their horse has already moved back to normal."

Birdie brought his horse alongside the conversation and shoved a big wad of chaw into his cheek which muffled his speech,

"Where'd they git to, Bodie?"

Bodie had a slightly disgusted look on his face as he stared at tobacco juice running down the boy's bottom lip.

"What?" said Birdie, as he swiped his chin with the cuff of his sleeve.

Bodie looked out over the grassy marsh, ignoring the boy,

"I figure there's three ways they could have gone; they could be headed for the other coast straight through the swamp, but I don't think so... It would take weeks to cross, and this man ain't done here. I don't believe it's in his nature to run, besides he wants Montgomery dead."

"For killing the woman and the boy; right, Bode?" asked Birdie.

Bodie ignored this and continued, "He could have entered the swamp and gone north or south, back-trackin' any wheres. Hell, he could be headed back to the home front while we're out here chasin' our tails."

"I could send two men south and two men north along the bank lookin' for tracks," suggested Big Joe.

"Nah," said Bodie. "It'll be dark soon and two men alone would be as good as dead if they come across him. I figure it's likely fifty-fifty we survive against him with ten of us."

Birdie squawked as if someone made a bad joke, "Come on, Bode, nobody's that good."

Bodie was getting irritated with the boy now, as was suggested in the sound of his voice, "You're not listenin', son. The legend of this half-breed is more truth than not. Git your ass over yonder and git to settin' up camp."

"Yes sir." Birdie knew when Bodie talked in that tone he'd better do as he said or somebody was getting a whooping. He turned his mare around, calling out to the rest of the men, "You heard the man, lets git 'er done."

Big Joe was the only one who stayed behind, he wasn't done talkin'. "The only option left is the hammocks."

"You're right, Joe, I'd bet my left arm he's holdin' up on one of 'em."

"It would take days to search all them out," reasoned Joe.

"That's why you and I are gonna' take shifts tonight with the scope on them there islands, lookin' for firelight or some sign of movement. Maybe, just maybe, we'll git lucky."

CHAPTER FIFTEEN

"Someone's comin'," said Walt from his position behind a downed cypress stump.

"One horse sloshin', movin' slow right for us," said Jebediah, "It's got to be him."

Chic, chic came the sound of Walt's rifle. "Well, if it ain't him I'm gonna' unload this here shooter in their ass!"

"Take it easy, old man," said Hunter from the darkness, as they rode in from the south side of the hammock. "Save your bullets for the bad guys."

The clouds parted at that moment, letting the moon light shine through. The water splashed as Hunter brought the Appaloosa up onto the limestone island from the knee-deep waters.

The old coots eased their triggers and walked over to the gunslinger and the lady.

"Jebediah, Walt, this here is…" Hunter paused.

The woman spoke up as he had hoped. "Helen, Helen Beckum. It's my pleasure."

"Howdy, ma'am," said Jebediah with a removal of his hat.

"Ma'am," followed Walt, pinching the brim of his hat between his thumb and index finger. "You son-of-a-gun; how the blazes did you git her outta' there with your scalp?"

"Walt!" exclaimed Jebediah, "I swear your mouth sometimes runs before your old mind can think it."

"He knows I don't mean nothin' by it. Hell, I kept me a squaw for ten year and she were ornerier than a wounded polecat. One time she..."

"Would you shush up?" demanded Jeb. "Now ain't the time for campfire tales."

Walt buttoned his lip reluctantly, long enough for Hunter to dismount and help Helen down from the Appaloosa's back.

"Come on," said Hunter. "We may not have much time."

He grabbed Zeke's reins and led him to their camp located at the center of the island, the rest following without reply. Once there, Hunter began digging through his saddlebags. He pulled out the spyglass and strapped on his gunbelt.

He talked while doing his ammo check, "Brush down Zeke, feed and saddle him, and git ready to head east."

"Well, that's the most sensible thing I'd heard yet," replied Jebediah. "Let's git the heck outta here."

"Helen will ride my horse. Move from hammock to hammock, stoppin' only at night, and no fires. There's enough jerky to git you to Lake Worth."

"You're not goin' with us?" asked Walt.

"I'll catch up."

"Catch up from what?" asked Jebediah, a hint of irritation in his voice.

"I'm gonna' take out that posse."

"And then?" asked Helen, her hands going to her hips.

Hunter looked at her and wondered if he would ever see her again. Looking away, he went back to his business of checking his guns.

"Me and Montgomery have unfinished business that's way past due."

"Even if you manage to take out the posse," reasoned Jebediah, "you can't take them all on yourself, son. Let us help."

"I don't mean no offense, but y'all will just slow me down."

"Please come with us," pleaded Helen.

The gunslinger made eye contact with her once more; he then turned and, at a run, he disappeared through the trees into the darkness.

"Well, I guess that settles that," said Jebediah reluctantly.

"*SHIT!*" exclaimed Walt as he took a brush to the Appaloosa.

"We can't just leave and let him do this by himself, against all those men," shouted Helen, her hands still on her hips.

Walt stopped brushing with a sigh and looked to Jebediah.

Jebediah stared back, a look in his eyes that unfortunately Walt had seen before.

◆❖◆

Hunter tapped into the Indian blood that ran through his veins, which was a gift from his mother, moving through the wilderness, unseen and unheard, like a predator. From his white father's lifeblood flowed his strength, determination, and nerves of steel – a gunfighter. The revenge he felt from lost loves was all his own.

He made it to a hammock closest to the camp where Montgomery's men were placed. It wasn't hard to find, for it was not far inland from where his and Helen's tracks ended at the bank of the swamp. The moon shone bright enough where he could see the men with his spyglass, through the trees and palmetto bushes. By moving his position several times, he counted eight men sleeping or resting. There were two men on watch; one of them with a telescope of his own. The man had it draped over the horse's saddle, looking into the marsh, sweeping from island to island .He was looking for firelight or any signs of movement, no doubt.

Hunter considered moving around this bunch and heading straight for Montgomery. These men would do one of two things. They would head out into the swamp after him, Jebediah, Walt, and the girl, or they would head back to the big house. Hunter did not need these men running up his backside while he battled the rest of Richard's hired gunmen. The half-breed made up his mind, he would have to take them out here and now, God willing. The waiting game would now begin.

Hunter looked up into the star-filled sky, gauging the position of the moon – just past two a.m. He would stay at the watch 'til four-thirty, allowing the men who would sleep to fall into it deep. He passed the time by whittling two spears from fresh cut, scrub oak branches, which he found growing near his position.

In these kinds of situations, there was always a plan, but it was always a short one. In an ambush, you could decide how to start it, but the middle and the end are decided on the reactions of the attacked. The attacker must then overcome and adapt – something Hunter could do very well.

Hunter looked to the moon through hundreds of bats that darted back and forth and up and down as they fed on mosquitoes. The bat was a sacred animal to the Indians; they were Mother Nature's bug exterminators. Hunter would rather have bats buzzing around his ears than the blood-sucking bugs that were particularly thick on this night. The men in the camp would find it difficult to sleep deeply as the insects fed on them with bustling annoyance, which could put his sneak attack in jeopardy.

The half-breed moved north through the grassy water for a hundred yards. Turning east, he made his way to the shore before turning south, through the brush toward the camp. Hunter was a hundred feet from the enemy when he stopped and removed his gunbelt and the shotgun from his side-shoulder holster. With the Bowie knife in his front belt, he put one 44 revolver in his belt at the back. Leaving the shotgun in the crook of a chest high scrub oak, he took the spears, one in each hand and moved swiftly, straight for the sleeping men.

Hunter's adrenaline was pumping and he could hear his heartbeat in his head, beating to the sound from the drums of Indian warriors of the past. He could see them lying there, unaware of what was coming. He ran at full speed past the first two who were motionless, appearing to be in deep sleep. The next two were moving. One was swatting bugs from his head; the other was changing position under his bedroll.

The decision was made. The half-breed thrust one spear into the chest of the one, the second spear pierced the stomach of the other. A third man, wearing red leather on his boots, sat up, startled by the cries of pain. With lightning speed, Hunter removed the Bowie knife from its sheath, grabbed the Red Leg's hair to pull his head back, exposing his neck. The warm blood sprayed outward as one slash of the blade opened the man's throat at the Adams apple.

The gurgling sound was suddenly masked by gun-fire as bullets whizzed by Hunter's head. He pulled his 44 pistol and slammed his palm down on the hammer, unloading his six-shooter. He killed two and hit another, spinning him to the ground. The gunslinger retreated out the other side of the camp running hard, back and forth, dodging bullets from behind. There were two, maybe three, in hot pursuit.

Hunter made a sweeping turn back toward his shotgun and gunbelt that waited patiently. He put more distance between him and the men with his deer-like speed. Hunter got to his guns with seconds to spare and strapped on his gunbelt then reloaded the empty revolver, sliding it into its holster. Down on one knee, facing his pursuers on the newly made path,

Hunter cocked back both hammers on the double barrel, took aim, and waited.

Seven seconds passed before two men carelessly came running down the narrow footpath. The gunslinger pulled the double triggers before the leader saw him in his low stance. They came down the trail single file. The front man in his hurried pursuit was destroyed by both barrels; due to his larger size, he screened the second man from the buckshot. The big man's body hit the ground, back first at the other's feet, stopping him in his tracks; the few seconds of hesitation allowed Hunter to drop the shotgun, pull his revolver, and put two bullets in the man's chest. Hunter waited for the smoke to clear and for the quiet to return to the forest. The one lay on top of the other. Their positioning would be humorous to some men, or tragic to others. The half-breed gunslinger felt absolutely nothing.

Hunter changed the cylinder out in his Colt for a full one from the right side of his gun belt. On the left side of his belt was where he kept his used loads, which varied in the number of bullets they contained. It was important for a gunslinger to know exactly how many shots he has during a firefight; keeping his weapons fully loaded at all times helped the memory count in stressful circumstances, which could mean the difference between life or death.

Hunter finished his reload then stood from his crouched position; he holstered his weapon to the sound of a hammer being cocked at his head.

"Don't move, mister, don't even flinch." The voice was high-pitched and a bit shaky. This one must have been behind him for some time before the silence returned to the woods, for Hunter would have heard his approach.

Birdie's mistake would soon be revealed to him. Hunter could judge the distance between them by feel. He dropped down and spun one-eighty into a leg sweep, knocking the boy off his feet. Birdie's revolver fell from his grip before he could get off a shot. Hunter was upon him in a heartbeat, pulling him up by the scruff of his neck and putting the Bowie knife to his throat. They stood there, perfectly still and silent, the boy's back pulled tightly to the half-breed's chest.

Hunter broke the quiet, "What's your name, boy?"

"Birdie..." It came out more like a low screech, with the blade pressed against his neck.

"Well, that explains a lot."

The boy thought he sensed humor in this man's comment.

"Are you gonna' kill me?" asked Birdie.

"I don't know yet. How old are you, boy?"

"I'm seventeen, soon to be eighteen."

"Sounds like you're in a bit of a rush to grow old. Drawin' down on me ain't no way to do that."

Suddenly, a rushing movement came from the brush. Down the path hurried a man Hunter recognized as the one who had a spyglass of his own. He held his pistol aimed right at them as he came to a stop at a distance of ten paces.

"Don't do it, gunslinger, don't kill the boy," insisted Bodie.

From Hunter's left a man appeared from behind a palm tree with a rifle in the crook of his shoulder, his eye running down the sight of the barrel and, no doubt, his finger was pressed against the trigger. He was moving sideways, slowly flanking the gunslinger. Hunter was turning with him using the boy as a shield and cutting off any angle that would give him an easy shot.

"Back off, Joe," commanded Bodie, "I got this."

"That boy is standing between me and a thousand dollar bounty!" shouted Big Joe. "I'm just in this for the coin."

Bodie yelled back, "I'm warnin' you, if you don't do like I tell ya, I'll shoot ya my damn self."

Big Joe came to a halt. Three seconds ticked by, he swung his rifle and fired at Bodie, but he wasn't fast enough.

Bodie had known Joe for many years and he knew his love for money was stronger than any friendship, so he anticipated his move. Dropping to one knee as the bullet grazed his hat, Bodie shot from the hip, hitting Joe just above his left eye, killing him instantly.

Bodie turned his revolver back toward the gunslinger and the boy.

"Nice shootin'," said Hunter. "Now drop the pistol."

There was a pause as Bodie seemed to be weighing his options.

"All right, all right," replied Bodie as he slowly set the revolver to the ground. "Just don't hurt the boy, he's only sixteen years old and my responsibility."

"Empty the other holster slow, and take a rest on that timber to your right there."

Bodie did as he was told. He pulled his other pistol from his gunbelt and set it next to the other. He looked to the left.

"Your other left," said Hunter.

Bodie looked to his right then slowly moved three paces and sat on the downed pine log.

Hunter removed Birdie's other pistol from its holster and stuck it in his belt as he spoke to the young man, "I'm gonna' take this steel from your neck. I want you to walk over there and take a seat with your partner there, got it?"

Birdie could not speak or even nod, the pressure and sharpness of the blade was too much, but they did understand each other. Hunter let him go. There was blood trickling from his neck, but the wound was shallow. The boy took the short walk and sat down next to Bodie.

The gunslinger retrieved the sawed-off shotgun from the forest floor without taking his eyes off his captors.

He came back to them while reloading the shortened twelve gauge.

Bodie gave the boy a bandana to dab the blood from the small cut on his throat.

"You cut me," complained the boy.

"Birdie, shut up," replied Bodie. His attention focused on the gunslinger.

"We hold no malice towards you, Mr. Dolin, we was just doin' our jobs."

Hunter squatted down in front of the two men, leaving a good distance between them before he spoke, "This must be the part where you try to talk your way out of this shit."

"Look," reasoned Bodie, "I hold no loyalty for Montgomery, It was just my work, and I had no idea you would be involved when we signed up. We can gather our horses and you'll never see us again."

Hunter grinned just a bit. "In my experience, in war you let prisoners go and they end up shootin' back at ya later on."

"At least let the boy go, I give my word he will ride outta this state for good."

"I won't leave without yah, Bode," said Birdie with conviction.

"You will do as I say, boy. Now pipe down and let the adults talk here."

Birdie stood up and threw the crumpled bandana to the ground.

"Sit down," ordered the gunslinger as he brought up the shot-gun and leveled it out toward the two men.

Birdie sat with some help from Bodie, who grabbed his wrist and pulled him downward.

"Look, I heard what happened to your family in Myakka, and knowin' Montgomery like I do, I'm sure he pushed it. We'll fight with ya; all I want is enough of the gold he's got on the second floor of that house so we can move on far away from here."

"You really expect me to trust you?" asked Hunter.

"We ain't no Red Legs," explained Bodie. "We're Crackers born and raised, If Matt were alive here today, he'd vouch for me?"

This last statement caught Hunter's attention. "How did you know Matt?"

"He was my late wife's second cousin, we grew up together. I met your pa a few times. I don't scare easy, but he was a dangerous man to git on the bad side of."

Hunter and Bodie locked eyes for some time; Hunter detected a look of hope in Bodie's eyes, while Bodie saw what he thought to be a look of ponder staring back at him.

"You're a good talker, mister," stated Hunter. "Besides, I don't know what else to do with yah. I'm not an executioner, but I am a survivor. Be warned, if I see any wide of the mark thoughts come across your eyes, I'll know it, and you won't even see me comin'."

"Don't you worry none, gunslinger," said Bodie with much relief. "We won't disappoint."

Hunter stood and put the shotgun in its side-holster. "Collect your weapons, we got travelin' to do."

"Well, all right then," said Bodie.

"Yes sir," said Birdie boy.

CHAPTER SIXTEEN

History was being made all across the United States as the North and South were engaged against one another in a bloody Civil War. As great men fought to unite their country – General Ulysses S. Grant who fought for the north and General Robert E. Lee fighting for the south – Richard Montgomery was fighting for himself. Buried deep in the swamps, he was carving out his own territory in a state that was left for the savages and cattlemen. He did not care about *God and Country*, only about his own power and wealth. His plan was working perfectly, except for one thing – a half-breed named Hunter James Dolin.

Richard Montgomery was on the second floor of his big house, sitting at his custom made oak desk; a beautiful piece anyone with any knowledge of good furniture would know had been built in the state of North Carolina.

He was three glasses deep into a bottle of Kentucky Bourbon as the sun began to rise. The man's demeanor was quickly deteriorating with every sip. He could not believe a half-breed rebel was threatening years of his sweat, hard work, and planning. The son-of-a-bitch just would not die. He slammed back the last of his drink and began pouring another, when there came a knock at the door.

"Come in."

The captain entered the room, ducking slightly under the doorjamb. He grabbed a glass from a serving tray on a table against the wall, and with a flip and a catch he set it down on the desk, rim side up. He spun a wood armchair around backwards and sat down on it across from Richard.

"Mornin', Monty, don't mind if I do."

Richard ignored the captain's rudeness and poured him a drink; he had bigger problems at the moment. "Any word from Bodie or the hunting party?" he asked.

"Aw-w, the Hunter is now the hunted, but for how long?" replied the captain before downing his whiskey followed by a wink. Then he slid his glass forward, indicating he would like another. "No, no word, but I would not expect one this early anyhow. I did some askin' around. You picked the wrong man to piss on."

"He's one man," said Montgomery through slightly clenched teeth. "A bastard, no less."

The one eyed sailor took the bottle from the table and poured his own, sensing he would not be served in an amount of time to his liking.

Richard watched the Captain with annoyance, waiting for his reply.

"This bastard is somewhat of a legend around these parts, and from what I can tell he's real hard to kill."

"What's the matter, *Captain.* You losin' your nerve?"

"No-no, I'm here for yah, Monty. All the men are in place and on alert. If we can just keep them sober, we'll be ready."

"Maybe we should send out a second revelry of men." suggested Richard.

The captain shook his head in the direction of no.

"The Seminoles call the half-breed *Lus-Tee Manito Nak-Nee,* means black spirit man, He's not goin' nowheres, he wants you dead, period. He'll come to us."

Montgomery stood up, the captain half-heartedly did the same. "I want *you,* Captain, to tell the men the bounty has just gone up: Two-thousand-dollars, in gold, for Hunter James Dolin's head on a stick."

"I'll spread the word. Gold has always been the best incentive to make someone dead. I might just go after him myself."

"Your job is to take care of *The Miss Lilly*," sternly replied Richard. "Which you have already been well paid to do."

"Don't you worry, Monty," replied the captain as he reached for the door handle. "My crew is ready and loaded for bear."

"That would be fine if we were huntin' bear, but we ain't huntin' bear, dammit." Richard followed the captain out into the hallway, "We need some way to flush him out into the open, some kind of trap, git him in a crossfire."

"What do you got in mind?" asked the one-eyed sailor, as he stepped aside allowing Richard to take the lead down the hallway.

"Come on outside and I'll show yah."

Their spurred boots clanked as they proceeded down the wood stairs to the first floor balcony at the back of the house that faced the lake. Montgomery was standing in the exact spot where he stood the night before, when Hunter had an arrow aimed at his throat. He had no idea how close he had come to meeting his maker.

It was mid-morning and cloudy with signs of rain. Montgomery stretched his neck and looked to the roof, where he could see two of the four men stationed there. Richard and the captain were standing by the railed stairs which led to the walkway to the dock, where the battle steamer floated proudly. Richard did not point as he spoke, in fear of being watched from a distance.

"We place a man with similar build and height as me, dressed in my clothes in plain sight, on the front deck of *The Miss Lilly* or the dock. If we can git the half-breed on the walkout between the dock and the house, we can hit him from all directions."

"I got yah," said the captain. "Men firin' from the roof of the house at his back with the Gatlin' guns firing from the boat to his front."

Richard looked out into the woods. "We put some men with rifles, spread out among the trees, staggered, firing at his side. If them damn fools don't shoot each other, I don't see anyone survivin' that kind of cross-fire."

"I'll see to it," replied the captain. "You got someone stupid enough to dress like you, and stand there like a goat tied to a post as bait?"

"I got just the Mexican. We call him dumb-dumb. I'm the boss and he'll do whatever I tell him to." Montgomery lit a big daddy Cuban cigar that he pulled from his inside jacket pocket. "If he's still alive, and he comes, it will be at night. It's to his advantage to attack in the cover of darkness. Let the men sleep in shifts during the day at their posts. I'll have Chinn deliver grub throughout the day. I want everyone rested and alert when the sun drops."

The two men went their separate ways to put the finishing touches on their plans. It would be a long hot day and even a longer night. Richard suddenly felt very long-standing; at this point he did not care about the outcome, he just wanted it over and done with.

CHAPTER SEVENTEEN

"Well," said Jebediah from his horse. "He's an easy man to track; he leaves dead men where ever he goes, like a trail of bloody bread crumbs."

"Jebediah, come look at this," hollered Walt as he was walking the grounds, his horse in tow by the reins held in his weathered hand.

Helen and Jebediah rode over to where Walt was kneeling and rubbing soil between his thumb and forefingers.

"There's blood here, not a lot. Over there," pointed Walt, "two men sat at that log side by side. They walked that way and collected their horses and left toward that away. This third set of tracks is Hunter's boots collectin' a horse here. He either got himself a couple of prisoners, or a tag-along."

"Hunter James ain't the type to take prisoners," commented Jebediah. "He must have recruited some friendlies," said Walt. "That would be good 'cause we can use all the help we can git." Walt mounted his horse. "Let's ride then. Jebediah, you lead the way; your eyes can track the ground from your horse better than mine."

Jebediah looked to Helen. "You ready to ride?"

"Don't you worry about me," she replied. "I'll keep up."

Helen was riding Zeke, the best horse of them all. She was wearing the dress she had grabbed when fleeing the big house. It was nothing fancy, which was good for riding. After taking draws from their water bags, they rode on.

Walt dropped back, taking up the rear putting Helen in the rocking chair of their little band. Jebediah led the way, only glancing to the ground occasionally. He did not need to follow the tracks; he knew exactly where the gunslinger was going. Jebediah did not speak it aloud, but he hoped revenge, disguised as justice, would prevail in the end.

◆ ❖ ◆

Hunter and his new companions were traveling single file, nose to tail, toward Montgomery's big house on Lake Okeechobee. Bodie was on point, Birdie second, followed by Hunter. The gunslinger had an advantage from his position at the rear, in case anyone changed their mind. Not that he particularly didn't trust his two new allies, it was that he didn't trust anyone completely. Hunter figured Bodie was only interested in the gold and a way out for him and the boy, With a price on Hunter's head, he might figure it easier to shoot him in the back than to fight Montgomery's small army. Hunter didn't really believe this, for Bodie seemed to be an honorable man for the most part, but he hadn't lived this long by taking chances.

They had burned up most of the day bringing themselves to a clearing where they now planned their next move from their saddles. Side by side, they discussed their options.

"I think me and the boy could do more damage from the inside," explained Bodie. "We walk right in with a story."

"What story would that be?" asked Hunter.

"The truth would work I think. We just change the end a bit. Me and Birdie boy here were the last ones left, we held you off, you fled, and we high-tailed it back."

"Are you sure Montgomery will buy that story?" asked Hunter, "Sounds unbelievable to me."

"You're the infamous Hunter James Dolin, killing all those men is not only believable, it really happened."

The gunslinger replied, not with arrogance but with a matter-of-fact statement, "I meant will he buy the fact that you two got away."

Bodie just stared at this man for a moment, waiting for him to smile as if joking, but it didn't happen.

"He's got a point," said Birdie, adding to the conversation for the first time.

Bodie suddenly realized the legend of this man did not only precede him, it hovered around him like a shield. Bodie had turned away from God when his family was taken from him. But now, he felt there was a purpose for this mission – something more than just gold. As righteousness crept into his psyche, the thought crossed his mind for the first time that the boy and he might just get out of this alive.

"Don't you worry, Mister Dolin. I can be very convincin', besides, I have been his right hand for some time now. He would just assume to believe me than to cut it off."

Hunter rubbed his chin in thought. "All right, Bodie, is it?"

Bodie nodded in agreement.

"Against my better judgment, I've decided to trust you two. I sure hope you all don't prove me wrong, 'cause I hate bein' wrong."

"You won't be wrong, gunslinger," said Bode. "Montgomery is a disease that has plagued this southern state far too long."

"What do you think, son?" asked Hunter, turning to Birdie.

"You askin' me?" asked the boy with surprise.

The gunslinger nodded.

"I've always done what Bodie told me, but I do have my own mind. If Montgomery did what everyone says he did, then he's got it comin'."

The plan was set; Bodie and Birdie boy would ride in and attempt to convince Montgomery the gunslinger had left the area, as far as they could tell. At first thought, Bodie wanted to tell Richard they killed Hunter, but without his body or his head this would draw suspicion to them. Richard Montgomery was not a trusting man; he was a clever and calculating sort. The simpler the story, the less information for him to calculate.

Once they were inside, Hunter would wait one night or maybe two before he would attack, hopefully catching Richard's army tired and off guard.

Bodie and the boy headed toward the home front.

Hunter positioned himself in a thicket just inside the tree line, where he could observe with the spyglass. He removed the Bowie knife from its sheath and carved a stand for the telescope out of forked branches from a scrub oak, aiming it at the point of Bodie and his boy's entry into the camp. This freed up his hands, allowing him to check his weapons.

Whether Montgomery believed the men's story or not, he would be idle for some time. Hunter would stay at his current position during the night, but before sunrise, he would have to retreat further back into the swamp to avoid detection. He planned to return the next night and begin his assault.

The gunslinger was not anxious in the least; he ate jerky for nourishment more than hunger. His mind drifted towards the memories of his old friend Mat, *"Your old ass would be happy, that I'm learnin' to work with a plan."* Hunter's thoughts were interrupted by movement and he checked the glass. In his circular view, he could see Bodie leading the way as they rode in under torchlight. Montgomery's men surrounded them, cocking their rifles and pulling the hammers back on their pistols.

"Easy, boys, it's me, Bode."

The men didn't fire, but they didn't lower their weapons either. Montgomery came around to the back from the front of the house; the same arrogance he carried on his face could be seen in his walk as he approached.

Bodie found it hard to believe that after all his men the half-breed had killed, Richard still maintained this demeanor.

"Drop those hammers, men," commanded Richard. "You three in the back there, douse them torches on the perimeter behind yah. The only thing easier than hittin' a sittin' duck is hittin' a well-lit one. Wouldn't you say, Mister Bodie?"

"Yes sir, *Mister* Montgomery," replied Bode.

The three men used their gloved hands to smother out the burning lamps standing upright in their holders.

"I'm sure as I could be that we weren't follered during the daylight, the last hour of night, I can't be for certain."

"Where are the rest of your men, Bodie? And more importantly where is my Lilith and the half-breed's head?"

"I'm sorry to say, the half-breed got away with the woman."

Some of the men could be heard and seen, grumbling and looking around nervously. Richards' brow narrowed with a look of distrust as he listened to Bodie's story.

"Me and the boy here just got plain lucky."

"And the rest?" asked Richard.

"All dead, sir."

"Explain, and it best be good, as you know my patience runs thin."

Bodie began to speak; Richard put his hand up palm first and insisted, "I want to hear it from the boy."

For the first time, Bodie felt a tinge of nervousness creep up his back. He looked to Birdie with a nod that said, *Well go ahead, and don't screw it up or we're both dead.*

"Yes sir, we were riding on the outskirts lookin' for signs, we heard gunshots, and by the time we got back to camp they were all dead. I ain't never seen nothin' quite like it."

"Oh, I have, son. I've seen first-hand what that savage is capable of. I just find it hard to believe you two somehow survived."

"Like I said," chimed in Bodie, "we got lucky."

"Yeah, lucky – I heard yah the first time." Montgomery and his right-hand man stared at one another for a few seconds, then was broken only by Richard's demands, "All right men, back to your posts. You two, come to the kitchen with me, get some hot food in yah, then I want to hear more on what went on out in that bog."

"Yes sir, Mr. Montgomery," said Bodie, as relief flowed through his body. He made sure that this feeling stayed masked within him.

Well, he bought it, for now, thought Hunter as he watched from afar. He made a decision right then to move deeper into the swamp, in case they made a sweep of the tree line. The gunslinger retrieved the horse he had borrowed from one of his well-deserved victims, and moved on, leaving his new allies to fend for themselves.

Chapter Eighteen

The moon was shining bright this night, giving off sufficient light for Jebediah and Walt to read the gunslinger's tracks. They both knew where he was headed anyhow, following his trail just gave them a more direct route.

"They split up here," said Jebediah. "Two horses went that-a-way, straight into the lion's den."

"I 'spect we got two workin' from the inside," said Walt. "If Hunter trusted them, I guess we will too."

"I don't see we have much choice in the matter," replied Jebediah. "But my name ain't Daniel."

"What the blazes does that mean?" asked Walt with annoyance.

"It means, I ain't just gonna' ride into that camp with the lions."

"Then what do we do now?" Helen asked from her mount, located behind the two men.

Jebediah ignored her for a moment. "We need to foller the single horse tracks off into the swamp and find Hunter. I don't think he'll be none too happy we brought the young lady along."

"I don't see how you two had a choice, unless you tied me up as a prisoner," Helen spouted.

"Don't think that thought hadn't crossed my mind, little lady," replied Jebediah. "Come on, we need to git movin'. It'll be daylight soon."

"Yeah," agreed Walt. "In daylight right here, we'd be sittin' ducks."

"Yeah," replied Jebediah, "then our goose would be cooked."

Walt chimed in, "That's a foul thought you're thinkin' there, Jebediah."

The two old men broke out in laughter as they followed Hunter's tracks deeper into the swamp.

Helen rolled her eyes, wondering if she was safe with these old coots – old *coots* – this thought tickled her, and she began to laugh right along with them. She realized she had not laughed in a very long time, and she rather enjoyed it. For the first time in recent memory, she felt hope for a new start on life. The gunslinger's image came into her mind, sending a tingling feeling down to her toes. Helen blushed as she put her hand to her lips with embarrassment. She thanked God for the darkness that hid her feelings from being known as she followed her new friends – in search of the man she realized she was already falling in love with.

◆❖◆

Just past sunrise Hunter James was having his morning meal in a clearing in the middle of some cypress. The ground was moist; as dry as you'd find in this part of the swamp. It was cloudy and fairly cool, storms could be seen and heard off in the distance. Between the peals of thunder, Hunter heard a faint but familiar sound. *Son-of-a-bitch.*

There was no doubt in his mind as the sound became louder and more frequent. They came through the cypress trees into the gunslinger's clearing, one after the other.

"What the hell?" asked Hunter, as he stood and walked over to Zeke and stroked his long nose as the horse whinnied again. Hunter looked up to Helen and their eyes locked. He noticed she was looking at him differently somehow.

"I told yah he wouldn't be none too happy," said Jebediah.

Walt attempted to explain, "We tried to do what you told us, but she is very stubborn and she has a rifle, she's younger than we are too..."

"Walt, stop," said Jebediah.

Walt gave Jebediah a glaring stare, but said no more.

"Well, there's nothin' to be done now," said Hunter. "You might as well eat. We got a long night ahead of us and we need to rest up."

Hunter's little army dismounted and joined him. The food was cold, for they could not risk the smoke from a fire. The gunslinger explained what happened at the posse's camp and the recruitment of his new friends. He told them of what he planned to do, the showdown would be tonight, and it was kill or be killed. Hunter could use the help, but he didn't want anyone doing anything they did not want to do.

"Are you sure you two are up for this?" asked the gunslinger.

"What the hell," replied Jebediah, "can't live forever. Besides, I figure killin' that Montgomery would be doin' the great state of Florida a favor."

"What about you, Walt? What are you thinkin'?"

"I'm thinkin' I'd rather drink turpentine and piss on a brush fire, but what the hell, I'm in. What am I gonna' do, ride out by myself like some coward?"

"What about me?" asked Helen as she looked to Hunter.

Jebediah and Walt looked to Hunter as well, for this was his show, and it was clear to them she was his woman, even if he didn't see it quite yet.

"We're goin' in on foot; I need you to stay with the horses just outside the tree line, in case things go badly."

Helen didn't protest, not even a little, for she knew this was going to be a bloody little war. She grew up tough and she knew how to shoot, but the men they were going up against were scraped from the bottom of the barrel. Helen knew this from experience, and Richard Montgomery was the worst. She would save her last bullet for herself, rather than fall into that man's rule once again.

They ate jerked beef, drank water from leather bags, and Walt and Jebediah shared a bottle of whiskey. When they offered Hunter the brew, he just gave a look. Without a word spoken, his steely eyes said much. The old warriors took one more sip and stored the bottle away. Ten hours before sunset, they would go into battle with a clear head.

Jebediah wondered if that was his last drink on this earth.

Walt did not even want to think about it, he just wanted a nap before the long night ahead.

Hunter would take the first and only watch of the day, for he could not sleep. He had been eaten up with revenge and anger for so long, like Montgomery, he just wanted it to be over. Hunter numbed his thoughts at his post at the tree line, by cleaning his guns. He swabbed each weapon of justice one at a time, so he would not be left unarmed. He cleaned one pistol, reloaded it, and then swabbed the other, leaving the shotgun for last.

As he pushed the wad of cotton through the 12-gauge barrel, he smelled her a half-second after he heard the crunch of earth below her feet. Helen sat down on a rise of lime rock protruding from the ground three-feet beside Hunter. He reloaded the shotgun and slid it back into its side-shoulder holster. He pulled out his cigarillos, unwrapped them from a thin sheet of deer leather, putting one to his mouth.

"Got an extra one of those, gunslinger?" asked Helen.

He handed her one, still not turning his head to look at her until he struck the match and put it to her cigar. He gazed upon her as she puffed on the smoke. It had been three or four days, and nights, since

Hunter had took this woman from Montgomery's big house, where he knew she was pampered. Living in the swamps for these many days had not left her any worse for wear. She was even more beautiful to Hunter somehow, more natural.

Helen glanced up making eye contact.

He looked away, guiding his attention to his cigar.

"Do I really look that much like her?" asked Helen, breaking a short uncomfortable silence.

"In some ways yes, and then again some ways no."

"In a few hours you're going to storm the castle, if you will, and life may be too short for you not to know how I feel about you."

Hunter was shocked, this he did not expect. He stood up and looked to Helen unintentionally.

She stood after him and took the two steps to face him. She took his hands into hers and, standing on the tips of her toes to reach his tall stature, she kissed him passionately.

At first Hunter did not kiss back, his mind reeling, then he could not help himself. He took her into his arms with passion. It was a long kiss, only broken by a twinge of guilt that crept into his mind. He pushed her away gently.

"Helen," Hunter spoke hesitantly, "I don't know if there is room in my heart for another."

"I have no doubt your heart is big enough, and I'm willing to share, for a while."

"You hit me with this, now?" The gunslinger took a few steps away from her, and looked around; making sure those old coots weren't listening in on this embarrassing conversation.

Helen sat back down on her rock. "I'm a woman who goes after what she wants. You will have a better chance to survive goin' into battle if you're fueled with somethin' other than revenge."

"So you came to me like this to fill my head with hope? Let me tell yah, hope to me is just an excuse to do nothin' – revenge has done well for me, thus far."

Helen just smiled at him from her rock stool.

Hunter continued, "All right, if you really want to help me, you can sit at the watch, so I can take an hour of shut eye." He pulled the shotgun from its shoulder holster and handed it to Helen butt first. "Just point and shoot, got it?"

"Got it," she said with a little salute. "Sweet dreams, gunslinger."

Lord, help me, thought Hunter, and without another word, he backtracked to camp where he planned to sleep.

After ten minutes of lying there listening to Jebediah and Walt snoring up a storm, he knew a nap was out of the question. He was kidding himself if he thought the nostril thunder coming from his two old friends was keeping him from rest. He knew it was Helen, and she was right. Killing Montgomery had been his only objective, but now – because of her – surviving was back on the card table. He thought about this woman as he drifted off to sleep while waiting for the darkness to come.

Chapter Nineteen

The gunslinger managed less than two hours of sleep, waking an hour before sunset. Helen was lying next to him sound asleep; his shotgun was leaning up in the crook of a small scrub oak. He picked it up, broke it for inspection, then slid it into the side-sheath. He watched Helen sleep as he checked his revolvers. She looked so young, beautiful, and innocent lying there before him. Another time, another place, he thought he would love this woman, but right now he had unfinished business to attend to. He could not start a new chapter in his book of life until he had finished the last. He'd been stuck on this page way too long.

Hunter's thoughts were broken by the rustling sound of Jebidiah as he made his way into the clearing.

"Where's Walt?" asked Hunter.

"He's on watch. He took over for the little lady here, bout' an hour ago."

"It will be dark soon," stated Hunter as he loosened then tightened the belly strap on Zeke's saddle.

"Yep," said Jeb, "the horses are saddled and ready to ride."

"How 'bout you, Jebidiah? Are you and Walt up for this?"

"Son, Walt and I have fought side by side for twenty years. We've killed Indians, Mexes', and anyone else we had to. This is just another one of those times – and if it's our last, then so be it."

"Don't you worry 'bout us, gunslinger," said Walt as he appeared through the trees, leading his horse by the reins. "We'll cover our end."

The undeniable sound of a rifle being cocked forced the men to react with a quick turn of their heads.

"I'll babysit the horses," said Helen, with her chambered rifle in hand. "But if anyone gets in my sights, I'm takin' the shot."

Hunter did not argue, he just looked upon her, and for the first time he truly noticed the toughness within this beautiful woman. "All right then," announced the gunslinger, "we ride with the settin' of the sun."

They finished packing their horses and raked the camp. With no fire to bury, the chores went quickly. Hunter used the last remaining hour of sunlight to carve out some arrows for his bow. Five crude sticks in all, but they would have to do. Hunter went over the plan as they worked.

When there was nothing left to say, they mounted their horses and rode in silence to the east, Straight for Montgomery and the big house. Helen looked back to see the sun setting into the swamp, wondering if this would be the last time she would ever see this beautiful sight.

The sun went down, setting another day behind it making the earth and everything on it another day older; reminding men that death is a part of life. Tonight, many would die before their time in an insignificant battle in the southern swamps of no man's land. As the Civil War raged on over states' rights, in the United States that weren't so United, an unknown battle was about to take place.

It was a dark night, the moon and stars masked by cloud cover, giving them a slight advantage to carry out their plan. They left Helen with the horses on a rise eighth of a mile from the Montgomery house; she was hidden behind a band of large pine trees. The torches at the house were hardly seen from this distance, it would be the only light to be seen in any direction.

Helen had her rifle and a pistol loaned to her by Walt, along with Hunter's spyglass. Her job would be hard, only to wait and pray for her men to return. She panned nervously back and forth with the telescope as she tried to keep the departing men in sight through the darkness.

Jebidiah and Walt were heading to the northeast, circling around to the back of the compound, while Hunter was moving to the west toward the lake. Helen followed Hunter as the men split up and she cursed as she lost sight of him when he entered the thicket. She panned around with the scope finally setting her sights on the firelight coming from the house; as she waited, she said a little prayer.

Jebidiah and Walt were playing the waiting game in their newfound positions, a hundred feet apart from each other. They were just inside the tree line at the back of the house, near the same area where Hunter and Helen had fled from a few days earlier. At times, the two old coots were dangerously close to the guards who roamed the compound, but they managed to avoid discovery by staying silent in their crouched positions while waiting for the signal.

Hunter made his way to the water's edge of Lake Okeechobee; he then cut his own path through the cattails 'til he found the spot he was searching for. From here, he could see the steamship, the main dock, and the well-lit boardwalk to the house. He could see three men on the dock and one on the stern of the ship manning the Gatlin' gun. His eyes followed down the long boardwalk to the house. Through the torchlight, he could see men armed with rifles on the balconies of all three levels.

Montgomery was nowhere to be seen, but with some insight from Helen, they figured he would most likely be held up on the second floor of the main house, surrounded by his men. Bodie and the boy planned to be close to Richard, with strict orders from Hunter to capture him if you can, but not to kill. Both man and boy agreed when they heard the signal, they would kill as many men as they could and leave Montgomery for the gunslinger to do with what he wanted.

Hunter removed his jacket and laid it to the ground on a dry spot along the bank. He unbuckled his gunbelt along with his extra ammo and set them, as well as the shotgun, on top of the jacket. He left his bow and arrows and stripped down to nothing but his fringed leather pants. The only weapon he took with him was the thirteen-inch Bowie knife tucked into his belt at the crook of his back. He waded out into the lake. The half-breed swam out past where the firelight from the dock could reach and quietly headed back toward the port side of *The Miss Lilly*.

Swimming underwater, he would pop his head up only long enough to take a breath and get his bearings. He did this several times 'til he reached the side of the ship. Hunter listened intently for any sound; then convinced there was no one close by, he shot up out of the water hands first, and grabbed the railing. Hanging from the steel bar, he now heard footsteps coming toward him. It was pitch black on this side of the ship with the wheelhouse blocking the light from the dock. Hunter hung there, perfectly still, as a guard walked by him no more than two feet away. All the man with the rifle had to do was look down to his left and he would see the gunslinger's hands grasping the rail.

Hunter held his breath as the thud of the boots faded away and there was nothing left but the sound of the wind on the lake. With one swift motion, Hunter pulled himself up and over the railing. Landing on his feet in a crouched position, water dripped from his body to puddle around his bare feet. He reached around and pulled the Bowie knife from his belt, stood, and headed toward the front of the ship.

When he reached the end of the wheelhouse, he heard the boot steps returning, so there he waited; five seconds went by. As the guard came around the corner, Hunter thrust the knife into his prey's throat. The man tried to scream, but could only manage a gurgling sound. Hunter laid the dying man on his back and removed the blade, the wood planks of the deck quickly turning red with blood. He left the body to twitch on its own and silently made his way to the stern of the ship.

Hunter heard a man snoring before he poked his head around the corner. Sleeping on a crate, he was leaning on the trigger handles of the Gatlin' gun. Hunter moved up behind the gunman. At once, the gunslinger slipped a hand over the man's mouth while piercing his side in an upward motion, the Bowie releasing blood from the kidney.

◆❖◆

Helen could barely contain herself, and the slight headache forming from the constant use of the spyglass did not help. By moving and changing her angle at the tree line, Helen spotted Walt and farther down she finally found Jebidiah at his post. From her position, she could not see the steamship or the dock, meaning she had lost sight of Hunter.

◆❖◆

Walt would have understood what Helen was feeling, for he was getting uneasy too, so much so he began mumbling to himself, "Come on half-breed, where the blazes you at?" And wishing Jeb was close enough to talk with.

Jebidiah was more patient then his two partners, but right now his anxiety level was at an all-time high. It had been a ways back since he had been in battle. He calmed himself down with thoughts of Walt, for he knew his friend was struggling more than he.

◆❖◆

As Hunter's friends were fighting the emotions of their inactivity, he was right in his comfort zone and about to blow this whole thing wide open. The man on the second Gatlin' gun at the front of the ship didn't go down as easily as the first. This soldier had been wide awake and at the alert. Due to the red leg coverings that the gunman wore, Hunter would enjoy this kill.

He was a step away when the bearded northerner turned to face him. As they struggled, Hunter's knife was knocked to the floor. The man was strong and determined, but it would not be enough. The half-breed swiftly put a knee to his rival's abdomen creating separation, and then with an upward motion Hunter slammed the palm of his hand into the man's nose, shoving it into his brain and killing him instantly.

The skirmish had been loud enough to alert the three men on the dock, and they ran for the ship. Hunter grabbed the Gatlin' gun, slid the hammer back, and then pulled the trigger. The gun kicked loudly with tremendous power as the bullets tore through the three men, shredding their progress. A mixture of blood and wood splinters mingled in the air on the narrow catwalk as they went over the rail to rest in the mud.

The gunslinger swung the big gun up and over, his finger never leaving the trigger as the large caliber ammo ripped through the back of the main house, along with the guards who had nowhere to go. He managed to clear the balconies of all three floors before the rounds ran out, killing many, and at the same time sounding the signal.

Hunter James ran down the back deck of the ship, put his foot on the rail, and launched into a dive over the side, disappearing into the dark lake water with a splash.

The captain and two of his men arrived at the side of the steamship's rail less than a minute after Hunter hit the water. They searched for a target, their guns at the ready. There was a slight ripple left behind but it was not clear enough to merit a shot.

Hunter swam as far as he could straight out into the shadows of the lake. Turning under the water, he surfaced just enough to exhale and take a breath and a look. He could see the three men eyeing his direction, but they could not see him. He took some air, went back under, and swam in a straight line to the south; he popped up for another deep breath before changing direction once again and heading for shore.

From the shallows, he ran to his weapons he left on the bank. Massive gunfire could now be heard, coming from the house. He knew he must hurry, for Jebidiah and Walt were outnumbered and engaged in battle. Not bothering with his boots or wears, he strapped on his gunbelt, the side-shoulder holster with the shotgun, and lastly scooped up the bow and arrows not wasting a single motion. He swiftly made his way through the woods toward the sound of shooting and the main house.

◆❖◆

Walt and Jebidiah tensely looked in each other's direction as the unmistakable sound of the Gatlin' gun began echoing through the swamp. Jebidiah was the first to fire; he cocked his rifle and killed a guard on the third floor balcony. Walt saw a man shoot in Jebidiah's direction; he aimed and fired, killing him from the bullet or the fall, as he went head first over the second story rail to the ground.

Two more men showed at the back, firing on Jeb. Bullets whizzed by his head and ricocheted off the trees he hid behind. Jebidiah wounded one, sending both men fleeing around the corner of the building.

Walt had his own battle going on with two others who rushed him at ground level. He shot from one knee hitting the closer of the two in the chest; the man went down. Walt cocked the rifle while swinging to his right and making a slight aim adjustment, then pulled the trigger; the old man's eyes widened when he heard the unforgiving *click* of his empty gun. Walt dropped his rifle and went for his pistol as the man fired hitting him in the shoulder.

Jebidiah heard Walt cry out; he couldn't see him, but he could see one of Montgomery's men barreling down on Walt's position. He aimed his rifle and shot the man in the cheek.

"Walt!" No answer. "Walt...! Answer me, dammit!"

"I'm all right, quit your bellowin'," grunted Walt.

"Are you hit?"

"In the shoulder... I'll live, but I ain't much use. I've got to git."

Their conversing was cut short as men fired upon Jebidiah from the south woods. "I'm a little busy right now," Jeb yelled in between shots.

At that moment, Helen appeared out of the brush on the Appaloosa and jumped down at Walt's side. She was helping him onto Zeke's back and taking fire.

Jeb finished off his immediate attackers and ran toward them, covering with gunfire as he went. He reached them quicker than his old ass thought possible, even killing one shooter on the run. Jeb helped them both into the saddle, smacking the horse on the butt and sending them off into the tree line. He turned in a panic, expecting to be overrun with men, but there was no one.

The concentration of the battle could now be heard coming from the lake side of the house. Jebidiah reloaded his rifle to its capacity and cautiously but swiftly headed in that direction.

Hunter had a total of five arrows he soon put to good use. He made his way from the lake to the tree line at the front of the house. The night remained very dark due to massive cloud cover blocking the light of the moon and stars. Hunter could see extremely well at night, taught to hunt in pitch-black conditions by the Indians of his youth. These men carelessly kept torches lit, up and down the catwalk from the house to the dock.

From behind a large cypress, the half-breed pulled back on his bow and loosed an arrow. It hit its target, in the side of one shooter's neck with only the duck feathers on the shaft keeping the arrow from exiting out the other side. The man fell with a *thud* on the boardwalk, dead.

Three men began firing blindly in the direction from which the arrow came; the cypress tree Hunter used for cover was being destroyed with bullets. He would have been pinned down if he was not already on the move. He moved toward the main house, continuously loading his remaining arrows, and letting them fly. He never slowed as he fired, keeping a deliberate pace; he aimed for the midsection of the gunmen, hitting one in the belly, another in the chest.

One man retreated, running down the boardwalk for the house. Hunter stopped and dropped to one knee then let the arrow loose. It hit the man high in the back shoulder as he ran for the front door.

Ten feet away from what he thought was cover, the door swung open and gunfire erupted from within. The arrow was no longer his concern as he was gunned down by his own. He fell backwards through a large puff of gun smoke, hitting the front porch with no less than twenty bullet holes gushing blood as the door was kicked shut violently.

A little trigger happy, aren't yah, boys? thought Hunter. He figured there must be at least four men holed up behind that door. He didn't think Montgomery was among them; he would be deeper inside, probably keeping to the second floor.

Helen had given him the low down on the entire building and he was convinced Richard would be in his quarters, surrounded by his best men, and, with any luck, his best men included Bodie and Birdie boy.

Two men from the third floor balcony spotted the half-breed and opened fire.

Hunter rolled from his knee and got behind a large pine as bullets whizzed by his head and littered the forest floor, much too close for his comfort. Montgomery's men had Hunter pinned down now, and they had the advantage from up above. Not to mention, he was in reach of the torchlight.

"Come on out, half-breed son-of-a-bitch," yelled one of the riflemen, with a crazy cackle. "We ain't gonna' hurt yah." He then fired repeatedly.

The bullets shredded the bark at the base of the tree where Hunter hid. He poked his head out very quickly to gauge the position of the shooter. As he did, another rifleman opened up on him; the splatter of tree bark stung his face.

Hunter had one arrow left. From a standing position, he stepped out from behind the tree and loosed it. The feathered stick hit the cackling fool just above the heart. The man dropped his rifle as he clutched his chest and barrel-rolled head first over the third floor railing. If the shot hadn't killed him, the fall certainly did. He landed on his head, bending his neck in an unnatural way.

"That'll shut you up," grumbled the gunslinger. He was so smitten with his handy work, he forgot to take cover – giving one gunman what he needed. Hunter was out in the open with an empty bow in his hand. The gunman aimed for his chest, a shot rang out. The bow fell from the gunslinger's hand, falling to the ground. Hunter jerked his head up to the roof were he saw a rifleman clutch his belly and stumble backward out of sight.

"You're welcome," said a recognizable voice.

Hunter, who had dropped the bow in favor of his Colt revolver, pointed it in the direction of the speaker.

Jeb stood in the forest twenty feet to his right, his rifle in his left hand and a smoking pistol in his other.

Hunter nodded in appreciation. "Where's Walt?"

"He was hit, but he'll live. Helen took him back to the meet-up spot."

"I'm goin in. You stay behind this tree and take out anybody you see, especially if they try to come in behind me."

"What about this Bodie and his boy?" asked Jeb, "I don't know their look."

"I suspect they're holed up on the second floor with Montgomery, playin' along. You just watch your ass, old man."

Talk was not Hunter's strong point, so without giving Jebidiah time to reply, he was off. Running to the catwalk, he jumped up and slung himself over the rail all in one swift motion. He pulled one of the torches from its holder and speared it over the handrail to the wet ground, extinguishing it as it stuck into the mud. He turned on his bare heel and dashed down the walk, grabbing the last burning torch between him and the house.

Walking straight for the front door, he drew the double-barreled shotgun from its sheath and one handedly pulled both triggers, blasting the latch. The door flew open, and in, breaking in half. Hunter tossed the torch through the opening and rolled head first along the porch floor, to the side of the doorjamb, just before the bullets flew.

More men came running around the corners from both sides of the porch, from back to front. Jeb opened up on the two closest to his side from the woods, unloading his rifle until they were both dead.

Hunter's Colt 44s thundered with smoke, as one man from the south fired upon him. The man did not expect the gunslinger to be firing from down low and he missed, aiming waist high the shots whizzed over Hunter's head. The gunslinger did not miss as his first bullet shattered the man's kneecap. As the man fell, the second lead ball went through his right cheek, exiting the back of his head with a spray of black.

Hunter scanned left and then looked right as he quickly loaded the shotgun then his pistols. He could hear men on the other side of the wall hollering and fumbling around. The gunslinger stood; clutching the scattergun, he turned and walked with purpose through the front door opening. His eyes quickly skimmed the room.

In the back area, two men were just finishing stomping out a small fire caused by the torch; they were unaware they had company. The two men to his right turned their heads to see the half-breed; eyes wide, they fired their revolvers. But they were hurried and one bullet whizzed an inch below Hunter's elbow, the other missing over the top of his right shoulder.

Hunter pulled both triggers, blasting them with the shotgun; their backs hit the wall leaving it bloody as they slid down to the floor in a strange sort of slow motion. The gunslinger dropped to one knee, pulled his pistol, and fired five continuous shots, slamming the hammer with his palm. The two men who had been fighting the fire didn't get off a shot. When the smoked cleared, the gunslinger was the only one still breathing.

He stayed down on his knee and methodically reloaded his Colts while he turned his head, looking over the entrances to the room and listening closely for the sound of intruders. Hunter released the revolver's lever, slid the pin, and replaced it with a reload. He had five full cylinders left in his belt, plus two others holding two bullets, one holding one bullet. He hoped he would not need to go to the partial reloads; if it came to that, it could be a short night.

Hunter stood and took the five steps to where his shotgun lay. He bent over, picked it up, and broke it open, replacing the spent cartridges. His shoulder strap was half-filled with shells, which was good – but he didn't have his jacket with the inside pockets that held extras. The gunslinger didn't dwell on what he didn't have – he was just making his count – like any good soldier would.

◆❖◆

Helen rode with Walt back to their safe zone and propped him up against a well-rounded pine tree for some doctoring. She'd already removed his shirt and was cleaning the wound by dumping whiskey on it and wiping around the edges with a rag of burlap.

"Ooww! *SON-OF-A-BIITCHH!*" yelled Walt.

"Take it easy, you big baby," said Helen. "It's just a scratch – well, its deep, but the bullet ripped clean through."

"Give me that, girlie," groaned Walt, as he took the bottle from her and took a swig. "This rot gut is better used sterilizin' from the inside." Walt slammed the bottle back once again; the gulping sound could be heard through the skin of his throat.

Helen grabbed the whiskey bottle from him in full tilt, spilling some on his mouth and chest.

"HEY!"

"Take it easy with that stuff, old man; I might need you if them scoundrels sniff us out back here."

"You know," said Walt, "you're so purty, if I were a younger man..."

"Save your energy, you flirt."

"What you'd call me?"

"Never you mind." Helen wrapped his shoulder with cloth she ripped from the hem of her skirt "Here, chew on this." She stuffed a wad of jerky into his mouth. "Don't swallow the meat, just the juice."

With a mouth full of dried deer meat, Walt dozed off for some much needed rest.

◆❖◆

"Hunter?" a whisper came from the doorway. "You still standin'?"

The gunslinger turned towards the entrance. "Come on in, Jeb."

Jebidiah stepped around and over the dead bodies as needed to get to Hunter's side. "I take it no one was up for surrenderin'?"

"That was their undoing," said the gunslinger in a matter-of-fact tone.

"Well, I saw three men ridin' east in a hurry. They weren't surrenderin', but retreat could add up to the same."

There was suddenly the *clomp* of boot steps and scuffling coming from the second floor.

Hunter pulled his pistols, cocking the hammers back with his thumbs. "I'm goin' up, Jeb. Clear this floor then meet me upstairs. And come in slow, but with purpose."

Jeb nodded in agreement.

Hunter headed quickly and quietly up the stairs, his bare feet completely silent on the wood steps covering his climb.

Jebidiah carefully made his way down the hallway, sweeping the first floor for intruders with his Navy Colt out in front and his rifle cocked and ready in the other hand. "All right you sons-a-bitches," whispered Jeb under his breath, "I'm a comin'."

Hunter reached the second floor hallway without incident. He moved to one of the closed doors where he was certain the sounds of struggle had come from. With a Colt in one hand and his Bowie knife in the other, he placed his ear to the wood. There was no sound; he took two steps back and kicked in the door, rushing in at the ready. In the middle of the large room stood Bodie and his boy, one on each side of Montgomery, their guns at his head.

Hunter's steel blue eyes locked on Richard's for a moment. There was a wood rocker in the corner of the room. He took a few steps and stuck the Bowie knife into the arm of the chair making it rock just a bit.

Hunter holstered his pistol and removed his gunbelt, setting it on the seat.

"I knew you were a coward at heart, *half-breed*," sneered Montgomery. "Got these *traitors* to do your dirty work."

"Bodie, back away," said the gunslinger as he returned.

Bodie nor the boy put their guns away, but they did slowly back up to the corners of the room.

Hunter was unstrapping the shotgun's side-shoulder holster when Jeb cautiously came through the doorway. He looked around the room, soaking it all in. "Hunter James, the first floor is clear, but there is still some men on the third, some on the grounds, and maybe on the roof."

The gunslinger said nothing.

"Just shoot him and let's git the hell outta here," Jeb suggested.

"All in good time," replied Hunter. "Just watch my back so I can do what I came here to do."

"Yeah, old man," said Montgomery, as he removed his jacket, then his button up shirt. "Do as you're told and when I kill this bastard Injun, I might let you live."

Richard Montgomery was older than Hunter, but he was extremely fit and well made, as if carved from granite. Ruthless and full of evil, he had no fear of death.

Hunter knew all this, but beating this man to death would help feed his hunger for revenge. Hunter did not fear death, either; he did not fear anything or anyone, but at this moment, a new concern crept into his mind – the concern of having no purpose at all.

What will I do when Montgomery is dead? A flashback of Lilith being shot in the head by this man went vividly through his mind. He then thought of Helen who was waiting for him according to her words.

Without another thought, Hunter took it to Montgomery.

He was four steps away from the older and slightly taller man, but it only took him two steps to reach him because Montgomery was bringing it as well, closing the gap by taking two steps of his own.

Their arms, fists, and elbows flailed and slapped with violent and blurring speed. First, Hunter pushing Richard back several steps, then Richard pushing Hunter back, back to the center of the room and to the beginning of the confrontation. They broke apart for a second, and then came at each other once again, same as before, but this time adding to their little dance, a vicious dance that neither man could decide which one should lead. Right away Hunter realized he underestimated this man, which was his mistake. Richard's arrogance was growing with his confidence, which could lead to his undoing.

Hunter made his move then; he swept Montgomery's leg and connected with a left palm punch to the chest, putting him on his back. Richard bent his knees as Hunter came forward, with his boots in his chest he launched the half-breed backward to the other side of the room, making separation, and giving him time to get to his feet.

Jebidiah was standing in the doorway, trying to watch the hall when he was not watching this amazing fight.

Birdie boy was armed on one side of the large room; Bodie was holding his rifle, keeping one eye on the window and one eye on the fighters. Bodie's anxiety was building, for he could see men in the semi-darkness down below, surrounding the house. His attention was brought back to the room as Hunter and Montgomery slammed into the desk beside him in a grappling tussle filled with left hooks and overhead blows. There blood showing on both men's faces.

A gunshot rang out; from Jeb shooting down the hallway toward the stairs. "Hunter!" yelled Jebidiah. "You need to quit screwin' around and finish this, we got comp—" He was cut short by the sound of a window shattering and there were now men firing from outside and down below.

Bodie ducked and covered his face from the flying glass before he could return rifle fire.

Richard Montgomery, with his back against the wall, reached down and grabbed his hidden boot knife. He brought it up and thrust down toward the gunslinger's face.

Hunter quickly dodged to his right, grabbed Montgomery's wrist and shoved the knife into his upper abdomen. Hunter used his body weight to pin him harder against the wall. The gunslinger could feel Richard's strength leave his body with the warm blood from his stomach.

"It can't be?" said Montgomery with a weakened voice, "I'm too young to die?"

"So was Lilith too young," replied Hunter. The gunslinger reached his hand out, "Bodie," and glared down at his revolver. Bodie pulled his gun from its holster and tossed it to him.

Hunter caught it; taking two steps back from Richard, he brought the gun up, pulling the hammer back with his thumb in one motion, and shot Montgomery in the head, splattering his brains all over the wall. Richard's body dropped to the floor. Hunter stood and stared down at the man that had absorbed his thoughts for too long. He waited to feel relief, or for something to fill the hole inside him, but there was nothing.

He had forgotten where he was and who was around him, until his privacy was suddenly broken by the metallic sound of triggers, followed by shouting men. The sounds of the room went from muffled to loud as he let his mind return. Hunter turned on his heel and leveled the revolver on a feeling, but he did not fire, there in the doorway was Jebidiah with the captain holding him from behind in a one-armed bear hug, his Navy Colt at Jeb's temple.

"Drop that hammer, gunslinger," demanded the one-eyed man.

"I got a clear shot at your good eye, and I won't miss," Hunter warned.

"I have no doubt of your skills, half-breed, but this Navy has a hair trigger. Now I think you need to back off three steps so we can talk."

After a pause, Hunter backed up slightly in front and to the middle of Bodie, who stood to his left. Birdie was behind him and to his right. Both men had their rifles raised, aiming at the captain.

"Easy, boys, not just yet," said the gunslinger.

The captain pushed Jebidiah further into the room, keeping him close. As soon as they cleared the doorway, two of the captain's men armed with revolvers entered quickly and fanned out, one on each side. The room suddenly got very small.

"Looks like we have ourselves a Mexican standoff," said the captain.

"Problem is," said Bodie, "there ain't no Mex'es in here."

"Maybe not, but there's plenty of Spanish gold in here, and that's what I'm after."

"That's our gold, you pirate son-of-a-bitch," yelled Birdie boy.

"Easy, Bird," said Bodie.

"That's right, boy, take it easy," replied the captain. "Well, it seems we all want the same thing, that gold in the other room." He then looked to the gunslinger with his one eye wide.

"What about you, Dolin, what do you want?"

"I got what I came for," said Hunter plainly. "Now, you're gonna let that man go. Y'all can split the gold, I really don't give a shit, but me and the old man are gonna walk out a here – or I'm gonna kill everyone in this room. My patience is growin' thin."

Jebidiah was impressed; he couldn't remember Hunter ever saying so much at one time. He did like the part where they walked out of there in one whole piece.

The captain looked to Bodie. "What do you say to that, Bode?"

"Whatever this man says is all right by me. What about them two?" Bodie's eyes, along with the end of his rifle, motioned toward the captain's men.

"They will do as I say. I will be taking the steamer and half the gold."

Bodie nodded in agreement, but he did not lower his weapon. Neither did anyone else in the room.

"How do we start?" asked the captain.

Jebidiah spoke up, the sound of irritation clear in his voice, "We start by gittin your pistol barrel off my head."

The captain released Jebidiah, allowing him to pick up his rifle from where he had been forced to drop it. He kept it to his side as he plopped down on the only chair still upright in the room.

"What about them?" called Birdie from one of the broken windows. "There's still a hand-full of armed men down there."

"What are they up to?" asked Bodie.

"Nuthin' much, just standin' at the ready."

"May I?" asked the captain.

Hunter nodded in agreement.

The captain holstered his pistol, his men did not. He went past them and entered through an archway that led into the other room. After a minute of rustling around, he returned with a wooden box, struggling with the weight of it as he walked it to the window. He kicked away the remaining glass and stepped out onto the balcony.

"All right men, you know who I am. Richard Montgomery is dead so that means your hire is done. This will cover any back pay owed to you. Take any horses, food and supplies, and move on."

The captain heaved the wood box and dropped it over the handrail. It hit the muddy ground with a thud and broke open, gold coin poured out the seams. The gunmen rushed over to the spot and began filling their pockets and satchels with the Spanish treasure.

The captain came back in through the large window with a grin on his face, to see the men in the room with their guns still leveled at one another.

"Gentlemen please, lower your weapons, I am a lot of things and one of those things is a man of my word."

Hunter lowered his 44 and picked up his shotgun, handing it to Jeb, who was still seated. "The old man here will oversee this little lootin' party, agreed?"

The captain nodded to his men, who lowered their rifles.

Bodie did the same, followed by Birdie.

Hunter watched as these killers in the room began acting like kids in a candy store. They put their differences aside, opened bottles of whiskey as they divided the loot, drinking and working together. Hunter grabbed a bottle, pulled the cork with his teeth, and chugged like a man who had just decided to jump from the wagon. He then dragged a small table over to Jebidiah and set the bottle on its top.

"Thank you, Hunter James," said Jeb smiling, before drinking like a man who had never even been near a wagon.

Hunter picked up the strap of shotgun shells and set them on the table.

"I'm goin' after Helen and Walt while you keep an eye on them. When that whiskey kicks in, things could change around here."

"I got yah, gunslinger. Hurry back – my old ass needs a nap."

Jebidiah saw the corner of Hunter's mouth move upward. It was more like a grin than a smile, which was the most you could get from this man.

Then the gunslinger was out the door as the early morn was being taken over by the sun beginning to rise from the east.

CHAPTER TWENTY

It was late August, or early September – Hunter wasn't sure; he figured maybe September, because of the dryer air and the light rain on the horizon. He had left the big house as the sun was rising behind a partly cloudy day. Down by the shore, he gathered up his clothes and after washing the blood off his body with the cool lake water, he dressed. Hunter looked up to see turkey buzzards circling overhead. They were preparing to feed on the dead bodies that littered the swampy grounds.

The gunslinger inspected the dead men as he went, a feeling of calmness spreading over him. He actually felt good, 'til dread came over him as Helen entered his mind. He quickly strapped down his guns by tying the rawhide strings on his legs, and took off at a run, inland to where Helen and Walt should be waiting.

Some of Montgomery's men spotted him at the back of the house heading into the swamp. They were rigging their horses for travel and loading them down with goods. One of the men reached for his rifle on the side of his black Cracker horse. Another gripped him by the wrist, stopping his progress.

"Leave it alone, Johnny. We got what we need – besides, there's no killin' that one. He's touched by somethin', and I, for one, don't want to find out what that somethin' is."

Hunter was well out of their rifle range as his continued run brought him to the edge of the woods. He ducked and dodged tree limbs as he entered. A hundred yards through the thicket, he broke into another clearing to find himself staring down the barrel of a rifle.

Helen dropped it and jumped into his arms, their lips locked in a passionate kiss.

"Oh, sure," slurred Walt from the base of his tree, "git me shot then steal my gal."

Hunter broke free from her, looking over her shoulder. "How is he?"

"He'll live," said Helen. "He's just a little drunk, that's all."

Hunter walked over to Walt. "Can you travel, old man?"

"Damn-n-n right..." replied Walt as he got to his feet and pitched forward.

Hunter caught him, sticking his hands in Walt's armpits, keeping the old man from falling flat on his face.

"Thankee sir, I mush a' tripped on a somin," said Walt.

"All right, let's git you on your horse. If I git yah in the saddle, can you stay there?" asked Hunter.

"Well, hell yeah, thish ain't my firs' rodeo."

Surprisingly, Walt did better in the saddle than on his own two feet. Hunter suspected the old man had done this many times before.

Helen was already on her horse, smiling and giggling at the spectacle of these two.

The gunslinger stroked Zeke's nose. "How you doin', boy? It's been a while." Before he mounted the spotted horse, the Appaloosa whinnied back in seeming agreement.

"Where's Jeb?" Walt demanded.

"He's where we're goin'," answered Hunter. "He's probably drunk as you by now."

Leading them through the brush, Hunter was feeling content, something that he wasn't used to. For a long time, he had not cared if he lived or died; he'd only sought revenge against Richard Montgomery and anyone who rode for him. Hunter was sure this time, all the men who were guilty for Lilith, the young boy Zeke, and Matt's death, were killed by his hand. He cared about life once again – he'd decided Helen would be his woman.

They arrived at the back of the house in a short time. The sun was two hours high, but completely covered by overcast skies. There was a chance of light rain, caused by a north wind blowing into the swamp for the first time this year.

Hunter and Walt glanced at the dead bodies with little thought. A flapping noise came from the trees and caught Helen's attention. She turned her head, looking around; to see the branches of the trees loaded with turkey buzzards. Up in the sky there were hundreds more circling the big house. In flight these birds were seen with beauty and grace, but up close their featherless skin-covered heads made Helen uneasy. She maneuvered her black horse past Walt, coming alongside Hunter.

"We must bury these bodies. It's the Christian thing to do, allowing those birds to tear them to pieces... I..."

Hunter interrupted her, "There's too many to bury. Besides, I'm not sweatin' over these scoundrels."

Helen gave him a look.

Hunter could not understand, but... "Maybe we could burn the bodies. Will that do?"

A voice interrupted their conversation, "I got a better idea."

Both Hunter and Helen turned in the direction of the speaker; Hunter doing so with his hand going to the butt of his revolver.

"Easy, gunslinger," said the captain, coming from around the corner of the big house. "Foller me, I got somethin' to show yah."

They dismounted. The short ride seemed to sober Walt up and, for the most part, he was able to walk on his own. It seemed his wound was not severe enough to keep a tough old coot like him down for long.

They entered through the same doorway Hunter had blasted in the night, where they came across more bodies. Walt stepped over one of the dead men with a grunt, holding his wound with the palm of his hand. "Looks like your handy work, gunslinger."

"They needed a lesson in manners, and I'm not one to put up with rudeness."

"Back here," called the captain from a first floor room, the sound delivered by a narrow hallway.

The large main room was dead center of the house. The captain's two men were sliding chairs and a table across the floor to the back wall, just under a painting of none other than Richard Montgomery. The picture had Hunter's full attention until the two men rolled up a fancy looking rug to reveal a large door in the floor.

As they gathered around, the captain pulled up the hinged wood trapdoor by a rope handle, letting it slam backward with a bang, uncovering the gator pit. The house set on pilings five feet above the water and the banging sound of the door brought the large reptiles to the center, looking for their next meal.

"These babies right here," said the captain, "will take care of the bodies without the burning smell and no one's got to dig."

Helen put her hand to her mouth and turned her head at the thought of the gators tearing the dead men to pieces. She walked out of the room into the hallway to gather herself. Helen was a little embarrassed with her reaction, for she considered herself a tough and worldly woman. She was leaning against the wall when Hunter appeared in the doorway.

"I'm fine," she said.

"We'll take care of this," said Hunter.

"You just make sure you put Richard Montgomery in first, so there's absolutely nothin' left."

Hunter smiled at this. "That's my gal – you are my gal, aren't yah?"

She smiled and touched his hand with hers. "We're gonna' leave this place, are we not?"

"Anywhere but here. We'll figure that out as we go."

"I'm gonna' clean myself up and pack my things, all right?" She turned and headed for the stairs.

"Hey..."

Helen stopped and looked back to him.

"Keep that shooter close by, there could still be unfriendlies here 'bouts."

She pulled her revolver from her belt and made her way up the stairs toward the third floor bedroom.

Montgomery went first into the pit; it took little time for the hungry gators to devour him and others. The problem was there were too many. The large reptiles could only eat so much, so the rest of the bodies were piled down-wind and burned. It was a dirty and tiring job, but it had to be done, and not one tear was shed.

CHAPTER TWENTY-ONE

In the late afternoon, Hunter and Jebidiah were sharing a bottle and smoking Cuban cigars out on the main dock. They had already washed and eaten from Montgomery's well-stocked kitchen. The gunslinger and the old man were armed and alert.

The captain had his two number ones on board the ship, plus three stragglers that had slowly appeared from the woods, their hands in the air.

The engines of the coal-fired steamboat were running as they finished loading the last of the supplies. The captain walked toward Hunter and Jeb while keeping his distance.

"Well, that's the last of it," announced the captain. "I guess we're done here and will be moving along."

Hunter noticed one of the captain's men appear with a rag and begin wiping down the Gatlin' gun at the stern of the ship.

"Do you think you can outdraw me, Captain?" asked Hunter.

"I've thought a lot about that, gunslinger, and I haven't decided."

Hunter's steel blue eyes pierced the captain's good one. "If you don't tell that man to back away from that rotator, I'm gonna decide for yah."

At that moment, Jebidiah cocked his rifle. While they talked, the man had dropped his rag and worked his way around to the back of the big gun, putting himself in a firing position.

"Thomas," yelled the captain, "leave her be – you can tend to your duties later on."

Thomas hesitated for a moment, and then he walked into the wheelhouse, out of sight.

"You greedy some-bitch," exclaimed Jeb. "You got a boat load of gold, and still you want more. You need to just git."

"Hey," replied the captain, his hands up and backing away toward the steamer, "an old pirate's habit dies hard."

The captain jumped aboard and unwrapped the last line from the bollard dock piling before shoving off.

Hunter and Jeb could see the one-eyed pirate grinning at them from the window of the wheelhouse as the steamship sailed away, the sky filling with white smoke from the stacks.

Hunter heard boots hit the walkout behind him; he turned to see Bodie and the young man heading toward them.

"Bodie and his boy is a comin'," said Jebidiah.

Hunter looked at Jeb. "Thanks for your insight."

"My pleasure."

"Tell me somethin', Jeb... What's that kid's name?"

"I-I'm not rightly sure, Bird...or somthin'."

The two had reached the head of the main dock when a large mouth bass hit the top of the water, scattering a school of shiners in all directions, temporarily diverted everyone's attention to the lake.

"If you don't think you need us," said Bodie, "we're all packed up and we'll be headin' out."

Hunter nodded in agreement.

"What are you gonna' do with this place?" asked Bodie "Burn her down, I expects."

"I hadn't figured that far ahead, to be honest with yah."

"Well, I have," interrupted Jeb. "Old Walt in there don't heal as fast as he use-tah, so I figured we'd stay for a while, maybe for good."

They all shrugged or nodded in agreement.

Without a word, Bodie and the boy turned and were several steps down the boardwalk, before Hunter spoke, "Thanks Bodie, and you too, Bird."

They stopped, turned and tipped their hats, then continued on, "Bodie?"

"Yeah Birdie."

"Will you call me just Bird from now on? I like that."

"Sure, kid," replied Bodie with a smile. "I think you've earned it."

Hunter, Helen, Jebidiah, and Walt ate a proper meal cooked by none other than Chinn Yang, who had been hiding in the house throughout the whole bloody battle.

The Chinaman asked them for a job.

After eating his cooking, and being served beer and whiskey by him, Jeb and Walt hastily agreed.

Following a generous amount of drink for all, Hunter and Helen retired to the third floor. They planned to leave first thing in the morning, but first things first...

◆❖◆

Several hours passed...

They held each other, unclothed and sharing a cigar while they discussed their plans, "Where will we go Hunter James?" she wanted to know.

"Where ever we want," said he. "There's a war goin' on to the north, so south maybe would be best."

"Whatever you say, Mister Dolin." said Helen as she snuggled up to him while making the purring sound of a cat.

"Keep that up," said Hunter, "and we'll git along just fine."

They both slept.

Hunter James Dolin was the only one to dream; Lilith came to him from the spirit world and kissed him gently. She told the half-breed gunslinger to live his life with this woman and be free for the rest of his days.

That's exactly what he would do. He would teach this young woman the ways of the gun and turn her into a gunslinger. Who knew what adventures they might find?

The End
(wanna bet?)

About the Author

Bret Lee Hart, a second generation Floridian, has spent the last twenty-five years in Marine construction; he is married and the father of two. His mother's maiden name is Emerson, as in Ralph Waldo, and on his father's side, Edgar Allen Poe can be found hanging on the family tree. With this bloodline of writers, and being named after Bret Harte from his western short stories, it was inevitable his imagination would find its way into print.

The *Half-Breed Gunslinger, Hunter James Dolin (Book II), Montgomery's Revenge (Book III), Wanted Dead (Book IV), and Wars End (Book V)* are the five books in this "cracker Western" series, as Bret calls them, and are available at major online book retailers.

The Fangslinger and the Preacher, Preacher Jack and the Fangslinger (Book II) are also available with many other adventures soon to be unleashed from this exciting storyteller's mind in various genres, including Fantasy and the Paranormal.

Follow Bret Lee Hart on Facebook:
https://facebook.com/bretleehart

OTHER WORKS AVAILABLE FROM BRET LEE HART

* * * * *

~ A Western action adventure, the first in
"The Half-Breed Gunslinger" *series ~*

In 1860 there was more open range cattle in Florida than in Texas and all the other states combined. It took a special breed of man to live there, and an even harder man to survive. Hunter James Dolin, half white and half Indian, was such a man. He was a gambler by trade and a gunslinger of necessity and attracted trouble wherever he traveled. But with his two Colt Walkers and bowie knife, he could handle almost anything.

Brief excerpt:
About ninety miles back and a few days earlier, in the crackerjack Saloon along the Withlacoochee River, Dolin's ace-high straight flush had beat one of the three outlaws' full house. He won fair and square – two ounces of gold and a just 'broke in' Henry rifle. These days that was more than reason enough to kill a man.

Hunter had felt the itch in his craw that warned him he'd out-stayed his welcome, and knew it was high time for him to leave this place. Without taking his eyes off the men at the poker table, Hunter had gathered up his winnings, while he spoke, "Thank you, Gentlemen. It's been a pleasure."

The man at the table to Hunter's left, the one who just lost his Henry rifle, had stood and replied angrily, "Do you think we're just gonna let you walk on out of here, half-breed?"

* * * * *

Spurred by revenge...
Gunfights and gold...
One man against the odds...

Hunter James Dolin survived the revenge war of Myakka City, Florida, by killing the men who raised their guns against him and his loved ones – all but one.

The Governor directed the Army to investigate, forcing the Half-Breed Gunslinger to seek refuge deep in the swamps of the Everglades.

Hunter James Dolin was content to live the rest of his life in solitude – 'til he was sought out and told of the whereabouts of the one that got away.

This would spark a new battle of revenge, overshadowed by the Civil War, but not soon forgotten by the people who inhabit the Florida swamplands.

Brief excerpt:
Scooter was swinging like a pendulum as very large Gators came up out of the water and snapped at the chicken, just out of reach of the man's head. Scooter was screaming again, as Hunter backed Zeke up a bit, putting his face and head closer to the teeth-laden jaws of the twelve-foot reptiles. The largest of the Gators stretched his neck up and snapped two pieces of chicken hanging down less than a foot from Scooter Johnson's head.

"PULL ME UP!!!! PULL ME UP!!!!" shrieked the dangling man. "I'm not the last – Montgomery's alive! *HE'S ALIVE, PLEASE!!!"*

Hunter urged the Appaloosa forward so the rope hanging over the branch moved with him, pulling Scooter up and out of reach of the Gator's bite.

"What do you mean, *he's alive?*" yelled Hunter. "I blew him up in his own hotel."

* * * * *

~ A Western action adventure, the third in "The Half-Breed Gunslinger" series, set in Florida. Author Bret Lee Hart reminds us his state was once as wild as the West – and just as deadly. ~

Duke Montgomery is an Indian fighter – a hard-as-nails killer, plain and simple – who doesn't think twice about ambushing a man or killing him face-to-face. When he learns his brother Richard is dead, killed by the Half-Breed Gunslinger, Duke goes on the hunt.

To avoid trouble after his dealings with Richard Montgomery, Hunter James Dolin and the woman, Helen, travel deep into the Everglades to live in peace for a while. But, as is the way of the world, trouble soon comes looking for them.

How many will die as Montgomery seeks the Half-Breed Gunslinger to get revenge? And what surprises are in store for Hunter James Dolin?

Brief Excerpt:
"Where you headed, mister?" asked Billy.

"Myakka City is my first stop," replied Duke.

"Where's that at, Billy?" whispered Junior, leaning toward Billy.

"Not sure," said Billy, "Where's that city at, Mister? Maybe we could tag along with yah?"

There it was; Duke had just recruited these two easily with his larger mind. He grabbed the whiskey bottle by its neck, and with the other hand chugged the last of his beer then slammed the glass mug on the counter. "We leave tomorrow mornin' at sunup, meet me at the hotel. You will be paid if you do your jobs and don't git yourself killed." Duke turned and headed for the door, taking his whiskey bottle with him.

"What might our jobs be?" said Billy to his back.

The shirtless, scarred, muscle man stopped and turned after two steps. "We're going to Florida to kill a stinkin' half-breed."

Billy and Junior looked at one another and grinned with confidence that the job would be easy enough.

"What do your friends call you, Mister?" Junior asked.

"I don't have any friends, but you will call me Sir." Duke turned and walked out, leaving the saloon doors swinging behind him.

✳ ✳ ✳ ✳ ✳

~ A Western action adventure, the forth in
"The Half-Breed Gunslinger" *series, set in Florida.*

While *The Half-Breed Gunslinger* fights for his life against infection from a gunshot wound, there are wanted posters being printed with his name and likeness. A $5,000 bounty on the head of Hunter James Dolin is more than enough money to attract men to the swamps of south Florida. The ending of the Civil War turns soldiers into bounty hunters as the North feels the need to cleanse the South, and men find ways to make a living.

The gunslinger's woman carries his child; Helen will need help from their close friends as her pregnancy progresses. Jebidiah and Walt will protect Helen at all costs with their experience and grit. Bodie and Bird, with their own skills, will be by their side in whatever comes their way. To their surprise, unexpected rivals come after the newly named Dolin Family.

Brief excerpt:
"What's goin' on, Hunter? Talk to me."
"Bounty hunter keeping track of our whereabouts." Helen's hand went to the butt of her gun. "Easy, woman; he's gone for now, but he will be back and with friends."
"What will we do?" she asked calmly.
"We can't stay here, it's too open. We could hold them off inside the cabin but for only so long; eventually they would burn us out. Myakka City is where our friends are; they will increase our numbers."
"Then we'll git little James, Alameda and Mocha and go to town at once."
"It ain't safe for the boy or you. I think maybe you should take little James and go with Alameda to the Seminole tribe lands..." Before he could finish, Helen was on her feet and shaking her head.
"I will not stay with that Sam Jones; Alameda can take little James and Mocha out there but I will go where you go." She turned and began walking up the bank to the cabin. "We best git packin'."
Hunter knew Helen meant to stand firm on her decision and there was nothing he could say to change her mind once she had made it. The boy would be safest with the tribe and Helen's skill with the gun would be handy. She had been battle tested and had killed without prejudice. She would be more dangerous now that she was a mother, like a mamma bear protecting her cub.

* * * * *

~ A Western action adventure, the fifth in
"The Half-Breed Gunslinger" *series, set in Florida.*

The three year Montgomery/ Dolin War was over, and not one family member named Montgomery was left alive. Hunter James Dolin had killed Richard Montgomery, his brother Duke Montgomery and their sister Jane Montgomery. The next man in line named Little Owl, for Chief of the Snake Clan of the Miccosukee, of the Seminole Indian Tribe was killed by the hand of the Half-Breed Gunslinger. Little Owl and his loyal braves were no more.

Myakka City and the James family had survived the last battle and Helen and little James were found alive at the waters' edge. Their current enemies were dead but Hunter was concerned about the wanted posters. There was no way to know how many had been printed and how far they had spread? The authors of the prints were dead but it would take time for this to be known and then believed. Five thousand dollars was a world of money and there would be men coming to kill the Half-breed Gunslinger and seeking their fortune.

Brief excerpt:
"The knife," said Hooker.

Hunter reached back and pulled the bowie from the sheath that was clipped to his pants at his back. Daryl took that too, with the same grin, only bigger.

"You take good care of that, Daryl; I will be needin' that back."

The stare of the gunslinger's steel blue eyes froze Daryl for a moment. His smile faded and then came back, but only a little.

"Oh, you won't need this no more, half-breed, not where you goin'."

"Daryl! I'm only gonna tell yah one more time to shut the hell up," the Captain warned. "Jimbo, tie his hands in the front; he's got to ride."

The big mouth drover picked up Hunter's pistol belt from the floor as Jimbo escorted the gunslinger outside. Zeke was there, and Hunter was placed on his back by two of the men.

"Where we headed, Captain?" Hunter asked.

"Daryl and Jimbo here will take you to Fort Foster and we'll let the army decide your fate."

"What of my family, Captain?" Hunter asked.

"When they are ready for travel I will personally escort them wherever they would like to go, unharmed. I give you my word as a lawman and a gentleman."

"You do as you say, Captain, Dand I will allow you to live. I give you my word, but your men here, a pass will not be givin'."

Jimbo glared at Hunter and Daryl laughed out loud.

"Let's go, tough guy," Jimbo replied.

"You try anythin', half-breed, and I'll kill yah with your own guns," Daryl said while resting his hand on Hunter's 44s that he now wore on his hip.

Hunter was glad to see his bowie knife tucked in the man's belt for he would need it as well on his return.

✳ ✳ ✳ ✳ ✳

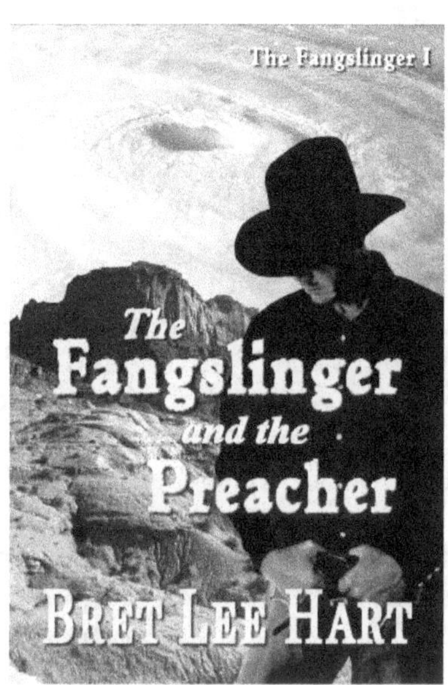

*~ A Paranormal Western based on the
age-old battle of good versus evil ~*

Master Andelko Balas is the leader of a bored, and therefore troublesome, vampire coven in Romania in the 1880s. Colonel Richard Andersson brings relief to the boredom by discovering tales of the American West and setting the coven on an exciting, but bloody, journey to a new land.

Jack Denton, reformed gunfighter, former preacher, now a drunkard, has visions of a great evil coming to Arizona as he wanders in the desert. Then he meets an Indian Chief and is given a silver sword, a special cross, and a mission. Jack is led to Black Mountain Mesa where an unusual storm is brewing and he has to face the greatest battle of his life.

Is this the last battle for the world as he knows it? Will his renewed faith and special weapons be enough to defeat such evil?

Brief Excerpt:
Black Mesa Mountain, Arizona, 1885
He went by the name Preacher Jack, given to him by his small congregation in New Mexico. He had buried the name Anderson in the past, going by the name Jack Denton in fear of being discovered by the law, or the lawless. It was a simple life he now led, and a good life for Preacher Jack, until God's plan for him continued forward. When his wife and daughter died from disease that swept through the small Mexican village, Jack lost his faith in God and left New Mexico, wandering aimlessly, not caring if he lived or died. Forty-year-old Jack Denton, a fallen preacher, was now a faithless drunkard living off whiskey – his only thoughts were of drinking himself to death.

Forty days and forty nights into his journey of despair, Jack found refuge in an abandoned mining shack to get some rest. A vision appeared to him as he slept, the drunken haze in which he slumbered left him, allowing the vivid images of his dream to come forth...

Fear overwhelmed him as something that Jack could only describe as a demon straight from hell swooped down on top of him, baring bloody fangs to devour his flesh.

Jack Denton awoke with a scream from the dirt floor of the mining shack.

* * * * *

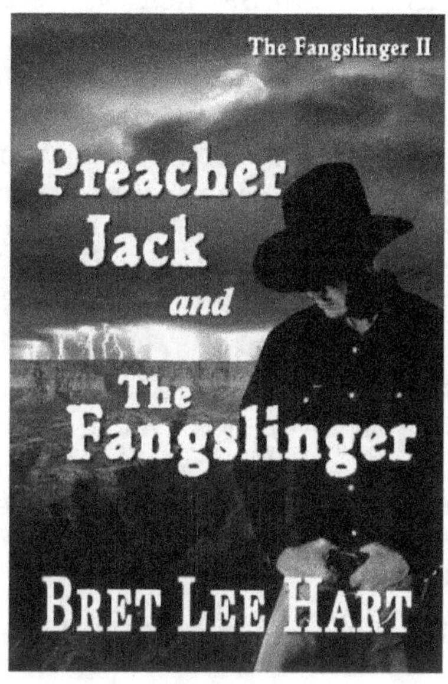

~ *The Paranormal Western sequel to*
"The Fangslinger and the Preacher" ~

Preacher Jack and his comrade Richard, a centuries-old Romanian soldier, thought their battle against evil was won after their climactic battle with the master vampire Andelko Balas at the top of Black Mountain Mesa. But Richard's former master was not vanquished permanently; the Fallen One has raised him up, and now Balas has an undead army at his command. The Preacher and the Fangslinger, aided by the mystical Indian White Owl and his followers, are now all that stands in the way of the vampire master's plan to empower his dark lord and unleash hell on earth.

Will the Preacher's faith be strong enough to sustain them?

Brief Excerpt:
On his return to camp, Jack was surprised to see that Richard had pulled himself up and was now leaning against a flat rock formation alongside the campsite that partially blocked the dry desert wind. As Jack got closer he could see that the color in Richard's face was much better. Jack then realized that the colonel had positioned himself in a shady spot to avoid the rays of the morning light. This concerned the Preacher, for this was something a man with the blood of a vampire might do.

"Does the sun bother you?" Jack asked.

"Slightly, yes," answered Richard, "may I bother you for some additional water?"

Jack fetched the canteen and went to one knee as he handed it over, but this time Jack did so at a greater distance.

Richard took several small sips, and then the two men stared at one another for a moment.

"You do not trust me so?"

"Ain't sure just yet," answered Jack, "you did save my life on that mountain, and the rumor is that we are kin, but the simple fact that you're hidin' from the sun does got me wonderin'."